"I've Tried My Damndest Not To Rush You, Tory

"But it's getting harder all the time to keep my hands off you. I keep thinking that sooner or later you'll admit there's something between us, but you won't...." Nick's eyes beseeched, even as they accused.

"There isn't any point in it," Tory said.

It was Nick's turn at incomprehension. "No *point* in it? What the hell's that supposed to mean?"

"Just what I said. I'm only going to be here for a year and you'll—"

"Don't deny us what we both want just because it can't last forever, Tory. We've got a year.... Let's just see where it takes us."

"I can't," she breathed, frantically searching for the auguments she couldn't seem to voice.

"How do you know?" His question was spoken against her lips. "You haven't even tried."

Dear Reader,

Welcome to Silhouette! Our goal is to give you hours of unbeatable reading pleasure, and we hope you'll enjoy each month's six new Silhouette Desires. These sensual, provocative love stories are both believable and compelling—sometimes they're poignant, sometimes humorous, but always enjoyable.

Indulge yourself. Experience all the passion and excitement of falling in love along with our heroine as she meets the irresistible man of her dreams and together they overcome all obstacles in the path to a happy ending.

If this is your first Desire, I hope it'll be the first of many. If you're already a Silhouette Desire reader, thanks for your support! Look for some of your favorite authors in the coming months: Stephanie James, Diana Palmer, Dixie Browning, Ann Major and Doreen Owens Malek, to name just a few.

Happy reading!

Isabel Swift
Senior Editor

SDRL-7/85

CHRISTINE FLYNN
When Snow Meets Fire

Silhouette Desire

Published by Silhouette Books New York

America's Publisher of Contemporary Romance

SILHOUETTE BOOKS
300 E. 42nd St., New York, N.Y. 10017

Copyright © 1986 by Christine Flynn

Distributed by Pocket Books

ISBN: 0-373-05254-5

First Silhouette Books printing January 1986

10 9 8 7 6 5 4 3 2 1

America's Publisher of Contemporary Romance

Printed in the U.S.A.

CHRISTINE FLYNN

admits to two obsessions—reading and writing—and three "serious" preoccupations—gourmet cooking, her family (she has a daughter and a husband she unabashedly describes as the sexiest best friend a girl could ever have) and travel. She tried everything from racing cars to modeling before settling into what she loves best—turning her daydreams into romance novels.

To Janet Gould

One

It had to be here somewhere!

Dr. Victoria Richards planted her hands on her hips and turned a slow circle in the middle of the weather-grayed cabin's storage room. The sparks of gold lighting the darkness of her brown eyes disappeared when her thoughtful frown encompassed the boxes piled everywhere. Well, almost everywhere. There was a bare spot next to a cot, and the shelves were half-empty.

Darn it! She'd had that book just this morning. If she could remember what she'd been doing before deciding to tackle the unpacking again, she'd remember where she'd left it.

You were silently swearing at the yo-yos who work for the moving-and-storage company, she reminded herself. Somehow they'd managed to ship three boxes full of old magazines instead of the cartons containing her medical supplies. Obviously those supplies were now in storage, along with her furniture. What was she supposed to do with five years worth of old *American Medical Journal*s and *National Geographic*s anyway? And how was she supposed to practice medicine without anything to practice it with?

Not wanting to start dwelling on that little dilemma again—and deciding to abandon the search for her book on yoga—she pushed a box of canned goods across the floor. Might as well do something productive instead of standing here stewing.

That thought didn't last long. Half an hour later she was leaning against the stepladder trying to figure out what to do with the boxes of muffin mix and cereal that wouldn't fit on the shelves. With a resigned sigh, she brushed her hands off on the seat of her jeans and shoved the boxes under the cot.

The muscles in her back protested when she straightened. It had taken a week of painting and scrubbing and beating out the beautiful hand-tied rugs covering the plank-board floors to make the cabin livable, then another three days to arrange the mismatched pieces of furniture the way she wanted and get most of her unpacking done. She was feeling every second of that exertion now.

"You're too old for this," she mumbled, pressing her hand to the small of her back. "Maybe you should've had your head examined after all."

The smooth line of her brow pinched. Good Lord! Was she talking to herself already? If she was like this after only ten days, what would she be like a year from now? Senility didn't usually strike at the tender age of thirty-two, but Tory was beginning to think she was a prime candidate. Who in their right mind would give up a position on staff at a prestigious hospital, a comfortable home in a respectable Los Angeles suburb and a Mercedes with less than five thousand miles on it to move to the Aleutian Islands?

Me, she said to herself, smiling—and the smile deepened when she recalled her chief of staff's flabbergasted expression when she'd strolled into his office six weeks ago to make her announcement.

She'd watched his incredulity turn to something bordering on indulgence while she told him about a third-year medical student she'd recently met. The student was Anton Nuclief, the eldest son of the mayor of a small Aleut village on Unalaska Island. Anton wanted to drop out of school and go back to his village. His people were in need of a doctor and he felt his knowledge was sufficient to care for them. Tory thought otherwise, and a slightly crazy idea had formed in the back of her mind.

Anton had only a year to go before he'd be minimally qualified. Why not go to the village herself? There were plenty of doctors in Los Angeles, but Anton's people didn't have even one. That meant his people's needs were greater.

If there was one thing Tory responded to, it was need. Besides, since Anton had so gratefully accepted her offer, maybe now she'd have the time to figure out what *she* needed—other than the shrink her boss had suggested.

Telling herself that what she needed right now was a cup of coffee, she headed into the narrow hall separating the storage room and her bedroom from the rest of the cabin.

Spring rain had again turned to snow, and a freezing wind whipped against her shuttered windows. It wasn't the racket caused by the elements that made her pause, though. It was the steady, droning sound punctuating the howl of the wind. Was it an airplane?

An instant later the sound was gone.

Just your imagination, she told herself, careful not to say the words aloud. Only an idiot would be flying in weather like this.

With a shrug, she tucked her almost shoulder-length black hair behind her ears and reached for the blue enamel coffeepot sitting on the wood stove.

The frantic pounding on her door ten minutes later was definitely not her imagination. Wincing against the blast of icy air that whistled in when she jerked the door open, she reached out to pull Anton's eleven-year-old brother, Willy, inside.

Willy looked like a miniature snowman. A thick pad of fluffy white flakes covered his sealskin parka, and his coal-black eyes peeked from the silvery fur trimming his hood. Instead of coming in, though, he was trying to pull her out.

"Dr. Tory," he panted, tugging on her sweatered arm. "You've got to come. A plane...two men... Dad says one's hurt bad."

In less than a minute, Tory had pulled on her boots and white ski jacket, yanked her thick white stocking cap over her head and was racing out the door. Seconds later, snowflakes were clinging to her lashes, the biting cold sucking the breath from her lungs. It was only by narrowing her eyes against the tear-forming wind that she was able to see Willy's sled with its team of six bushy-tailed malamutes standing next to her woodshed.

Tory's feet had no sooner planted themselves on the hide-covered vehicle than the crack of Willy's whip sent the sturdy and surprisingly fast team of dogs lurching forward.

"Slow down!" Her startled cry was tossed back in her face by the arctic wind. Landing on her bottom with a jolt, she grabbed the reed-thin side rails and hung on for dear life.

The Aleutian Islands, those tiny dots of volcanic soil erupting in an arc between the Pacific Ocean and the Bering Sea, suffered some of the most unforgiving weather in the world. Not a single tree grew here, and only a few scraggly tufts of dead grass interrupted the windblown mounds of white. Those mounds had to be rocks, and Tory could have sworn that Willy hit every one of them as he pummeled them toward the edge of the frozen sea.

Trying not to think about what the tooth-rattling jolts were doing to her backside, Tory peered through the blowing snow. Shadowy figures had loomed into focus. There were a little more than two hundred people in the village and, from the looks of the crowd gathering at the shore, at least half the male population had already arrived.

The instant the sled slowed, Tory bolted to her feet. The Dorvak brothers rushed past, having left their flock of sheep to offer their assistance. Behind them came two seal hunters. The Aleuts were a good and protective people. In an emergency, everyone helped.

Dear God, she prayed, swallowing a lungful of frozen air as she hurried through the snow, please don't let this be something I can't handle.

Her skills were excellent, but there were times when skill meant nothing unless the proper equipment was available. She hadn't exactly packed the Mayo Clinic in the cartons she'd so carefully filled and labeled, but they had contained the essentials. Damn those moving men, anyway!

A twin-engine Cessna, its nose resting precariously on solid white ground and its tail bobbing in the broken ice of the ocean, sat a hundred feet away. Cargo boxes were being hastily unloaded. Ropes were being thrown this way and that. Through the blustering snow, she saw a limp figure being lifted from the plane by three of the men.

She recognized two of those men as villagers by their gray sealskin parkas. The third man was a stranger. He was a good head taller than the others and looked like a great golden-headed bear in his heavy Sherpa jacket. The tone of his commands and the sheer physical strength betrayed by his lithe movements indicated that this stranger—the pilot?—had taken charge of the frantic activity.

The ground lurched under her feet just as she reached the nose of the plane. It wasn't on solid land after all, and the ice was breaking up. The spring thaw had already begun and the plane's impact had hastened the disintegration of the six-foot layer of ice.

Refusing to panic, she took a tentative step forward. The ice tilted.

She barely had the chance to think that maybe a little panic wouldn't be terribly imprudent when the stranger darted toward her. A split second later, she was crashing into his very solid chest. Her cheeks, already numb from the cold, felt hot against the snow clinging to his jacket.

"Get out of here!" came his impatient command as her head snapped back. "I've got enough trouble without having to fish you out of the ice!"

Her gloved hands had instinctively locked on his arms to keep herself from falling. "I'm trying to help!" she shot back, and jerked her hands away, only to grab for him again. The ice insisted on pitching at odd angles and she tried not to think about the fact that nothing more than the giant ice cube she was standing on separated her from God only knew how many feet of burning cold water.

Before she could raise her eyes to the face she'd yet to see, she was being turned and pushed in the opposite direction. "The best way for you to help is to stay out of the way. You haven't got enough muscle for seal bait."

She whirled right back around. "I didn't come to unload—" *the plane,* she finished to herself. He was already jogging off.

Hunching her shoulders, she followed him toward the figure the other men had carried a safe distance away. Had he actually thought she'd listen to him? "Cretin. Neanderthal," she muttered, then skipped a few millenium to add, "Nerd."

A group of men hovered over the injured passenger. The stranger reached them seconds before she did, but his attention was being temporarily distracted by one of the villagers who'd rushed up and was pointing toward the plane. She took advantage of his preoccupation by squeezing in between Stephan Dorvak and Willy's father, Albert Nuclief. Dropping to her knees, she pulled off one of her gloves and pressed her fingers to the injured man's neck. His pulse was strong.

Her breath of relief, which was audible only to herself, met with the man's groan as his eyes fluttered open. "Don't try to move," she instructed, her glance sweeping the awkward angle of one stocky limb. Adding a note of lightness to her tone—a practiced method of reassurance—she quietly continued, "It looks like you've tried to rearrange the structure of your leg, but we'll have you—"

"I told you to get out of here!"

Patience, she warned herself, and calmly lifted her head.

Brown eyes that revealed an arresting combination of vulnerability and quiet strength met challenging ones of pale blue tinged with green; eyes the color of the sea and whose depths revealed that same awesome turbulence. For the briefest instant the challenge faded to something almost quizzical before flicking over her face in an assessment so thorough Tory forgot to release the breath she'd just inhaled—and about the prone figure she was kneeling beside.

She jerked her head down, unable to fathom her lapse in concentration. "Several times," she said by way of dismissal. "Albert?" Not giving the stranger a chance to start yelling at her again, she asked Albert to help her find something to support a broken leg—a couple of slats from the wooden crates being unloaded from the plane would do—and then to have the men bring up one of the sleds.

Albert was nodding, but not at her. He seemed to be silently telling the stranger with the aquamarine eyes that it was all right for him to leave his passenger. When Tory turned to add her own assurance, the stranger was running back to his plane. Someone had just shouted, "These ropes aren't going to hold!" and within seconds he'd joined the men piling crates onto the rocks.

It was several minutes before the injured man—Craig, he said his name was—was wrapped in sheepskins and strapped to one of the long, bowlike sleds. It would be a cold, uncomfortable ride for him, but it couldn't be avoided.

What could be avoided was another confrontation. And a confrontation seemed to be exactly what the man heading toward her had in mind, if his scowling expression was any indication. Now that his cargo was safely out of the badly listing plane, he must have decided to take another shot at her.

It was as good a time as any to head back to her cabin. Tory hated arguments, especially when there was no reason to argue. Since she'd have to go back the same way she came, she started to look for Willy.

"Wait a minute!" Bending his head so he could be heard, the stranger stepped in front of her. "Just who in the hell are you? And—" a gloved hand waved toward Craig "—where are they taking him?"

Over the bansheelike scream of the wind, Tory shouted, "I'm a doctor. And they're taking him to my place just outside the village." Narrowing her lashes as much against the sting of ice crystals pelting her face as his furious scowl, she encountered those incredible eyes. "Are you the idiot who was flying that thing?"

It was impossible to tell for sure, but she thought a slight flicker of amusement darted between his impossibly long lashes.

"What if I was?"

Good point, she conceded, and watched him plant his hands on his hips. That gesture made her feel every bit as small as her five feet four inches was next to his six foot two or three. She shouldn't have called him an idiot.

Albert came hurrying toward them before she could say anything else she might later regret. "We're ready to go, Tory. Willy'll take you back." Turning to face the man beside her, he continued, "Everett will see that your equipment is taken to the hall, Nick. You can come with me. We don't have much room, but you're welcome to share Willy's bed."

Tory's eyes slid from the stranger—Nick—who was nodding, to Albert. Her brow pinched. Albert knew this guy?

Obviously, she thought to herself, tossing a curious glance in Nick's direction when she started to move away. Albert was already walking off, but Nick wasn't following.

Something about him halted her own progress. He was standing very still. The look in his eyes was unfocused, almost glazed, and his firmly chiseled lips were suddenly as white as the landscape.

"Are you all right?" The question was barely out of her mouth before she realized how stupid it was. Of course he wasn't!

He pressed his hand to his head, seeming to summon the strength from somewhere to remain upright. "Of course I am," he snapped, managing to sound impatient even though he'd little more than mouthed the words.

He started to sway.

Tory reached for him just as his knees buckled. A hundred and ninety pounds of heavy male muscle sank toward her, crashing against her slender frame and slamming them both to the ground.

"Albert!" Gasping for the air that had been forced from her lungs, she tried to ease herself from beneath the limp weight. "Albert!" she cried, louder this time. "Hurry!"

Scooting to her bottom, she cradled Nick's head in her lap. He'd obviously been hurt in the landing, yet he'd insisted on helping with his passenger and unloading that fool airplane. "You really are an idiot, Nick-whoever-you-are," she muttered at his inert form, and hunched forward to protect his face from the wind.

Well, he did seem a little short on common sense, not to mention stubborn. And what about arrogant? That, too, she thought, then decided that as long as she was going to sit here pinning labels on him she might as well be fair about it. She had to admit that only someone with a very unselfish sense of responsibility would have overlooked his own injuries to make sure his passenger was safe. The cargo could have waited, though. At least until—

The screeching groan coming from behind her was joined by the sound of ripping metal. Tory canceled her last thought. She didn't have to turn around to know that the plane had just sunk.

It took Albert, his nephew and the two Dorvak brothers to transport the injured men to Tory's cabin. After assuring herself that Nick the Idiot probably had only a minor concussion, if that, she had the men deposit him in her bedroom. She needed the cot in the storage room for Craig. His leg could be elevated with some of the boxes.

Since the crate slats weren't long enough to use, Craig's leg was set in a makeshift splint constructed of planking and a blanket. Definitely not pretty, but good enough to stabilize the break. Making him as comfortable as possible, she left him with Albert and headed into the hall. Albert's nephew and the Dorvaks had just left.

She paused when she reached her bedroom door.

Unlike the plasterboard covering the walls of the other rooms—every one of which she'd painted—the walls here were rough wood. Homespun beige curtains covered the long window opposite an old, age-patined dresser. The large feather bed with its gleaming brass headboard was the nicest piece of furniture in the place. It was that bed she was looking at now—rather, its occupant.

Nick seemed to be sleeping quite soundly. His jacket had been removed and a red-and-black flannel shirt covered the rhythmic rise and fall of his broad chest. A pair of well-worn jeans stretched over his narrow hips. Pure male—and looking even more so lying on the luxurious fur coverlet the villagers had given her as a welcoming gift.

She moved her eyes back to his face. It was impossible not to notice the sensual fullness of his slightly parted lips. Or the length of the wood-brown lashes closed beneath the heavy slashes of his eyebrows. Thick golden-brown hair tumbled over his wide forehead, and there was a tiny cleft in the point of his strong chin. Even in sleep, his jaw was held in stubborn determination.

Shaking off her less-than-clinical appraisal, she moved to the side of the bed. He looked all right, but he'd taken quite a bump on his head and she had to be sure he hadn't suffered any other damage.

Tory deftly unbuttoned his shirt and tugged it from his waistband to push the fabric aside. Her medical mind noted the perfect formation of pectoral muscles covered with a fine mat of curling brown hair. A more primitive part of her saw only a broad sweep of fabulously formed chest. He had to be the most incredible specimen of masculinity she'd ever seen—from a purely medical standpoint, of course.

Gently, so as not to wake him, she pulled the shirt over his shoulder. Her eyes narrowed at the angry red bruise running along his collarbone. Good grief, she silently moaned. What else had he done to himself?

"Craig's asleep now," Albert offered quietly from the doorway. "Do you need any help here?"

Matching his near whisper, she nodded. "Please. He's hurt his shoulder, but I can't tell if that's all. If you could help me get him out of these . . ."

Between the two of them, they managed to divest Nick's long frame of his clothing—everything except for his jockey shorts, anyway. Through it all, Nick didn't budge. Either he'd slipped into a coma, which she doubted, or he was so exhausted an earthquake couldn't have roused him.

Resolutely avoiding taking in the whole of him, Tory's fingers worked skillfully over his arms and chest seeking further injuries. Nothing seemed to be broken. Just that awful bruise, and a goose egg on the side of his head. Better to have the swelling relieve itself on the outside, instead of in.

"I take it you know these men, Albert?" She glanced at the weathered man who'd treated her like a member of his family since the day she'd arrived.

All he did was nod and look back at Nick.

With a shrug, she moved down to Nick's legs. Thick muscle and sinew barely gave beneath her expert touch. For some inexplicable reason, it was taking every ounce of her considerable self-discipline to keep her mind on her medical duty. Legs were legs. Skin was skin. So why did the silky-coarse hair slipping under her fingers seem to sensitize her fingertips and...

Good God, Tory, she admonished herself. This morning you were talking to yourself. Now you're imagining things. Just remember what this guy's like when he's awake! "There're some plastic bags in the drawer next to the sink in the kitchen, Albert. Would you get one and fill it with snow for me?"

If Albert was puzzled by her request, nothing in his expression revealed it as he hurried from the room. Lifting her hand from Nick's calf, she straightened—and two large hands shot out, locking around her wrists.

An instant later, she found herself sprawled halfway over the length of Nick's body. The momentum snapped her head forward and her startled gasp repeated itself when she felt his lips against her temple. Her head jerked back.

"You didn't have to stop," he chuckled. "What you were doing felt nice. You give back rubs, too?"

Mindful of her Hippocratic oath—adding another knot to his head would be a little unethical—and far too aware of his warmth permeating her sweater, she scrambled to her feet.

"I see you two finally met." Albert, trying to hide his smile behind disapproval, set the snow-filled plastic bag on the carved wood nightstand. "But just to make it official... Dr. Victoria Richards, I'd like you to meet Dr. Nicholas Spencer."

Under normal circumstances, Tory would have extended her hand. Considering what had just happened, she wasn't about to. Something told her she'd probably find herself flattened out on top of him again. "Doctor?" she inquired, sounding considerably less surprised and shaken than she was.

The man lying on the bed gave her a wide smile, the devilish grin making his already attractive features even more appealing. "PhD. Not medical," he supplied. He turned his head toward Albert, trying not to wince with the movement. "If this is the woman you were telling me about, you managed to omit a few details. She doesn't look anything like the doctor you described."

"I thought you might see her differently. You people have a saying." Albert gave Tory a wink before returning his attention to Nick, whose attention seemed centered on the cabled pattern of the sweater covering her gently rounded breasts. "I believe it goes something like 'Beauty is in the eye of the beholder.'"

"Ah, yes." Nick's eyes narrowed first on Albert's broad, flat features, then on Tory's remarkably calm expression. "I suppose by Aleut standards she is a little pale. She's got nice cheekbones, though. The nose is probably too delicate, but the mouth isn't bad." His glance traveled approvingly from her neck to her knees and back up again. "I'll refrain from further comment. She doesn't look like she's ready to deck me yet, but no sense pushing my luck."

The man was astute. Very astute. Even though his appreciative look refuted his words, she didn't find his teasing particularly flattering. Somehow he'd made her sound like the runt of the litter.

"You're going to have a headache for a day or two," she quietly advised, and watched the smile that had started to form on his lips turn to a frown. Obviously he'd expected more of a reaction from her than he'd got. "And your shoulder's going to hurt for a lot longer." Without quite understand why, she would have loved to make sure his head hurt for at least a week. So he made a pass, she said to herself with a mental shrug. Big deal. This wasn't the first time something like that had happened. "Do you hurt anyplace else?"

She saw his mouth tighten just before he mumbled, "No."

"Good. Don't move around too much, and try to sleep if you can. Albert, would you help him under the covers, please? When he's settled, give him that ice bag." She nodded toward the nightstand, then directed a benign, professional smile to the cleft in Nick's chin. "It'll make your head feel better. I'll be back to check on you in a while."

There was no reason to run, but Tory had to make a conscious effort not to while her long, graceful strides carried her to the stove in the kitchen half of the cabin. Grabbing the pot, she poured herself a cup of coffee and promptly burned her tongue with the first sip. "Damn," she muttered, testing her tongue against the back of her teeth.

Pulling up one of the three stools by the pink Formica counter that cut the twenty-by-thirty-foot room in half, she plopped down on its hard surface.

She hadn't felt a thing when Nick had pulled her down and his lips, accidentally or otherwise, had brushed her temple. The knot that had formed in the pit of her stomach was only the result of ... of shock. He'd startled her. And the slight difference in her heart rate when she'd first encountered those gorgeous eyes was only... Well, whatever it was, it didn't matter anyway.

Not exactly convinced that she was buying her own logic, she blew across her coffee and took a more careful sip as she watched Albert's stocky frame emerge from the bedroom.

He stopped by the counter. "Will they be all right?"

Tapping her finger against the side of her cup, she watched the steam curl over its rim. "I think so. Craig needs to be taken to Anchorage or Kodiak as soon as possible, though. His leg has to be X-rayed and casted. As for Nick—" Nick was as strong as an ox "—I'm sure he'll be fine after he rests for a couple of days. Do you want some coffee?"

Albert shook his head, his straight black hair brushing equally black eyebrows. "Katrina's got supper on by now and I'm sure she wants to know what happened. I'd better go soon."

His soft black eyes left her face to glance around the familiar room. He hadn't been inside the cabin since the day she'd arrived.

When Tory had first seen the cabin, her initial response had been a slowly moaned, "Oh, my God." She'd expected rugged, but the mental pictures she'd created weren't quite as rustic as the real thing. Unlike her home, which she'd done all in white with strong accents of bright yellow, this place was...well, the U-shaped kitchen half of the room had those pink countertops, and the curtains above the sink and in the living room were a rather bilious blue. The living room was actually the area on the other side of the counter. It contained a heavy wooden sofa covered with brown tweed cushions, end tables that had probably been made in the year one, two rickety ladder-back chairs that held each other up by the wall next to the door and a large, colorfully braided oval rug.

In spite of the fact that nothing went with anything, after she'd been here for a few days she had to admit that the place had character. There was even a certain coziness about it. Maybe it had something to do with the warmth coming from the big black cook stove that was the only source of heat.

Albert felt the coziness for another reason. This cabin had been his mother's and would be his oldest son's when Anton returned to the village next year.

"It's good to have someone living here again." His voice was gentle as always, a perfect reflection of his manner and that of his people. "Why aren't you using the electricity? Is something wrong with the generator?" His gaze had settled on one of the kerosene lamps glowing softly against the pale blue walls.

A sheepish smile curved her lips. "There's nothing wrong with the generator. It's just sort of noisy, and I like the lamps."

"My mother preferred them, too. But she used seal oil instead of kerosene."

Tory watched Albert's eyes and sensed his approval. The Aleuts spoke with their eyes, their soft darkness more telling than their quietly spoken words. Albert had told her that the eyes were a reflection of the spirit, the essence of one's belonging with nature.

"Albert? You said you know these men." Hoping he'd be more receptive to her inquiry this time, she propped her elbows on the counter. "Since they're both going to stay here tonight, I'd like to know who my houseguests are."

"Of course you would," he agreed, looking for all the world as if it was the first time she'd mentioned the subject. "Nick heads up an exploration team working with geothermal energy, seismic activity and the like. He was here for a while last summer and then again a couple of weeks ago to find a place to set up their base. He's finally decided to put it over on Umnak, but he asked me to radio Anchorage and have the rest of his crew wait. They were supposed to meet him there tomorrow. Can't tell you anything about Craig, though," he added. "Never met the man before, but if he works with Nick, I'm sure he's fine."

Nick definitely had a champion in Albert, if the admiration in Albert's expression was any indication. Tory preferred to draw her own conclusions about the man, though. "When you call over to Anchorage, would you radio for a medical pickup, too?"

"Nick already asked me to," he said, backing toward the door. "But I'm not sure Craig will want to get into a plane after the way he landed his today."

Albert left minutes later, after explaining how the unpredictable spring weather was no match for even the most seasoned pilot. That brief explanation—and the realization that Nick hadn't been flying the plane—left Tory frowning down at her cup. Now she really wished she hadn't made her earlier reference to Nick's mental capacity.

For the next several hours, she tiptoed between the rooms the two men occupied. Craig's sleep was restless and she wished she had something stronger than the aspirin she'd given him for his pain. The only other thing she had was a menstrual-cramp reliever. That probably wouldn't help much, but maybe she'd try it the next time he woke.

Nick, on the other hand, had barely moved a single, glorious muscle. Even when she wakened him every fifteen minutes to check his pupils, he'd just mutter at the intrusion and promptly drift off again.

It was almost midnight before she finally found a comfortable position between the lumps in the sofa—relatively comfortable, anyway. She was freezing. With everything that had happened, she'd forgotten to get more firewood from the woodshed before nightfall. There was only one log and a few pieces of kindling left by the stove. If she used them now, there wouldn't be anything to start the fire with in the morning. It always seemed coldest in the mornings.

Sticking her nose under the collar of her ski jacket—the men had all the blankets—she prayed for the oblivion of sleep. She was denied her request by the quiet male groans filtering from down the hall.

At first she thought it was Craig, but he appeared to be sleeping quite soundly now. As she passed her bedroom again, she heard Nick's muffled voice.

In the pale arc of light thrown by the kerosene lamp she held, she saw his golden head tossing back and forth on the pillow. Each movement brought another moan.

Though it was definitely chilly, he'd kicked off the blankets and the thick fur coverlet, exposing one muscular leg and the breadth of his chest. The sheets rustled as he flopped over on his side.

If her guess was right, he was reliving the crash he'd experienced that afternoon. It must have been terrifying. No one could go through something like that and not have it affect him somehow—even if it was only on a subconscious level. She should wake him. Then she'd cover him up and go back to her spot between the lumps.

Shivering from the chill seeping through her jeans and sweater, she set the lamp on the nightstand and bent to tug the blanket from between his legs.

"What the...?" His words trailed off with a groan.

"It's okay," she assured him softly. "You were dreaming."

The sound he made was a cross between "Huh?" and "Oh."

The sheet was tangled around his ankles. "Move your leg."

"Where've you been?"

"In the other room. Move your leg." Since he didn't seem to understand her request the first time, or this time, either, she reached down to push on his calf.

He sounded a little more coherent. "Your hands are cold."

"Sorry. Can you lift up? You're supposed to be under the blankets, not—" she gave another tug "—on them."

"I can if you'll stop frowning at me like that. I don't eat little girls." There was an unmistakable note of teasing in his sleep-husky voice.

"I'm not frowning at you." She really wasn't. Her eyebrows had just scrunched together when she'd pulled on the blanket. "And I'm not a little girl."

"Then maybe you have something to worry about after all."

If he was feeling good enough to tease, he'd obviously suffered no ill effects from his dream. "The only thing I'm worried about right now is getting you covered up and me back to the sofa so I can get some sleep."

"Sleep sounds good. Lie down."

"What?"

"I said, lie down. Your hands felt like ice, and if the way you're shaking means anything, the rest of you is just as cold."

"My coat's warm enough." The jacket she'd slung over her shoulders did keep the top half of her body warm. It was the bottom half that was threatening to suffer from frostbite.

"Do you have a blanket out there?"

"No, but—"

"You'll be warmer here. You won't do yourself or Craig any good if you come down with pneumonia. So, stop talking and get in." He moved over, pulling back the blankets she'd just straightened.

She started to take a step backward, but it was canceled even before her mental arguments could be voiced. His fingers gently grasped her wrist, pulling her down to the mattress. "Come on," he coaxed. "My head's pounding and I don't have the energy to argue with you."

Him argue with her? She was the one who needed the rebuttal! But she was tired. And the bed—*her* bed—looked so inviting. He'd moved all the way over to the other side, and that would leave a good three feet between them, so...

Making a mental note to double the amount of firewood she usually brought in during the day, she pulled off her boots and crawled in, all but clinging to the edge.

"You don't have to stay over there," he said, and she felt his arm curve over her waist to pull her to the middle of the bed. Her eyes widened when she felt him fit his chest neatly to her back. "Your sweater scratches."

"It's wool." Picking up his arm by the wrist, she pushed his hand back to his hip.

His arm flopped back over her waist. "Feels more like porcupine quills."

Was he going to ask her to take it off?

Apparently not. Seconds later she heard the sound of his deep, rhythmic breathing. He'd already fallen back to sleep.

Two

___

Tory was vaguely aware of a tickling sensation on her nose. She breathed in a clean, slightly musky scent, her half-conscious mind thinking how nice it smelled, and snuggled deeper into the solid warmth. There was an unfamiliar weight, a very pleasant heaviness, draped over her legs and something that felt comfortably protective circling her waist. A sense of security seemed to pervade the other sensations, making the dull gray light teasing the back of her eyelids an unwanted reality.

Her eyes reluctantly fluttered open.

Oh, my God, she moaned to herself and, willing herself not to move, held her breath. Was he still asleep? Could she possibly disentangle herself and get up before he woke? Her eyes felt gritty, but she didn't dare move her hands to rub them.

Her hands! One was curled up between her and Nick, and the other was curved against his back. And his hand was moving up between her shoulder blades.

"Morning." The husky greeting was spoken to the top of her head.

"Morning," she mumbled into his chest. So much for a clean getaway. "Ah...how's your head?" Well, she hastily rationalized, what else are you supposed to say when you wake up in the arms of someone you just met?

"Better. But it still hurts a little."

"Do you want some aspirin?"

"Maybe later."

He shifted, bringing their intimately aligned bodies closer. She was already aware of the formidable bulge pressing against her lower stomach. Did he always wake up with a...? "How's your shoulder?" Better to think about other parts of his anatomy.

"How does it look?"

She pulled her head back just enough to glance at his shoulder but not to see his eyes. She didn't think she could handle that just yet. "Bruised," she replied flatly.

"That's how it feels. You sleep okay?"

"Yes." She might as well ask, too. "You?"

"Better than I have in a long time."

Funny. That's just what she'd been thinking.

The warmth of his breath feathered over her forehead, and his hand was moving in small circles between her shoulder blades. That motion seemed almost a reflex, as automatic as his breathing.

Biting down on her lower lip in an attempt to divert her mind from the very pleasant feel of his fingers tracing over her sweater, she drew her arm from his waist. "I think I'd better get up now."

"You can get up in a minute. You married?"

Talk about a major change of subject! "No," she swallowed.

"Albert said you've been divorced for a few years, but I just wanted to make sure. I don't like sleeping with married women."

Meaning that he did sleep with them but didn't necessarily prefer it? "All we did do was sleep, Dr. Spencer. Now, if you'll move your leg..."

"Don't you think the 'Dr. Spencer' bit is a little formal? After all, we did spend the night together." She was absolutely certain he was grinning. "Aren't you curious?"

"About what?"

"Whether or not you spent the night with a married man."

She really wished he'd stop putting it like that. "Did I?"

"No. Never could see committing myself to something that wouldn't last anyway."

"That's an interesting philosophy." She managed to sound dismissive, even though she couldn't help but wonder at such a negative attitude. Despite the fact that her own marriage had failed, she still had a very healthy respect for the institution.

"Let's just call it a conviction," he suggested. "How long have you been here?"

The man sure knew how to play conversational leapfrog.

"This is ridiculous," she muttered.

"What is?"

"This conversation." And the fact that they were lying here talking as if they woke up together this way every morning.

"I don't see anything ridiculous about it," he countered, teasing. "A little unusual. Possibly even unique. Or maybe—"

"I get the picture," she mumbled with a groan.

"Good. Now, how about an answer?"

"A little over a week."

"Quite a change from California, isn't it?"

Her eyes widened on the dark brown hair swirling at the base of his throat. "How did you know where I was from?"

"Albert mentioned it. I've never lived in California, but I did spend a year on the Baja peninsula, so that was pretty close. That was before I went to Greenland, though. Looks like home will be here for the next few years."

It sounded as though home was wherever he was at the moment. If what Albert had said was right, Nick would be spending the next three years over on the next island. Not that it mattered. She wouldn't be here that long.

Something drifted over the back of her head, the touch light, almost caressing. "I like your hair," he said, sifting it through his fingers. "It feels soft."

Last night he'd said the shape of her mouth wasn't bad, either. A soft smile curved that mouth, then vanished. She didn't care what he'd said. This was ridiculous! "Will you please let me up now?"

"Why? Aren't you comfortable?"

There was no way she could answer that. It wasn't a question of comfort at all. "I need to check your friend."

She'd been trying her best to ignore the tingling that had formed a knot in the pit of her stomach. It was a slightly electric sensation caused as much by his lazily moving hand as the hard feel of his body.

That knot constricted when his fingers tangled in the thick fall of ebony hair tumbling behind her neck. With a gentle tug, he eased her head back to rest in the curve of his arm. Incredible jewel-colored eyes smiled down at her.

It was those eyes and the fact that his lips hovered mere inches from her mouth that made her throat go dry.

For God's sake, Tory, a voice cried inside her head. Get up!

She tried to move. At least she thought she did. But there was something lurking beneath his heavy lashes that was having a decidedly unnerving result. Her arms and legs simply refused to obey the commands her brain was frantically issuing.

The corner of his mouth quirked in a teasing half smile. She wished he hadn't done that. All that little smile did was accentuate the creases carving vertical lines in his lean cheeks.

She didn't doubt for a second that he was fully aware of the effect he was having on her. He'd probably debilitated half the female population of the western hemisphere with that deceptively boyish expression. Boyish? He was probably close to forty!

"Checking on Craig—" he lowered his voice to a seductive whisper "—is the only excuse I'll accept."

With that, he pulled his leg away and rolled over to his back.

It was only Tory's ability to remain calm in a crisis that allowed her movements to be unhurried as she climbed out of bed and headed for the dresser. And what had just happened *had* been a crisis of sorts. For a moment there she'd thought he was going to kiss her, and for that same moment she'd actually wanted him to.

That man's your patient, she snapped at herself, not really sure what that had to do with anything, and glanced over her shoulder when Nick asked, "Where'd you get that?"

More disconcerted than she'd admit by the smug smile he couldn't quite suppress, she turned back to the low knotty-pine dresser. "The balalaika?" she returned, identifying the triangular, guitarlike instrument propped up in the corner by the bed. "I bought it in California."

It was silly to feel so relieved at how calm she'd sounded. She always sounded that way.

There was a puzzled note in Nick's voice though; one he seemed to cover with an offhanded observation. "Since some of the people here are of Russian descent, I thought one of them might have given it to you. It's a Russian instrument, isn't it?"

Rummaging through one of the drawers, she pulled out a blue sweater and a white turtleneck jersey to wear under it. The wardrobe that had once sported the labels of Dior and Halston had been replaced with the more practical Levi and Wrangler. "I think so. I'd never even heard of it until I saw a rerun of *Dr. Zhivago*. Ever since then, I've wanted to learn to play."

"Are you very good at it?"

"I don't know. I haven't learned how yet." A clean pair of jeans was pulled from another drawer. "It's a project."

"Is yoga a project, too?"

Slanting him a glance that had "How on earth did you know that?" clearly stamped on it, she saw him leafing through the book he'd picked up from the floor by the nightstand.

So that's where it was. She'd been so busy swearing at the movers while she'd stuffed the old magazines under her bed that she'd forgotten where she left it. One of her colleagues had become interested in yoga a couple of years ago and Tory had finally decided to give it a try. Inner peace and tranquility were promised to those who could master its mental and physical aspects. Tory was all for that.

"Among others," she returned, scanning the top of the dresser for a ribbon to tie back her hair.

"Such as?"

She couldn't decide if he was just a naturally curious person—which any good scientist would have to be—or if he was trying to make up for acting like such a jerk yesterday. His present mood was certainly an improvement, even if he was looking at her as though she amused him somehow.

"Such as how to grow things. Would you excuse me, please?"

"Sure. Where's my shirt?"

Patiently pushing a handful of sleep-tousled hair from her face, she picked it up from the chair by the door. While he'd certainly be warmer dressed, he was to stay in bed. She was preparing to tell him that when she handed him his shirt, but Nick didn't give her a chance.

His eyes had followed her hand when her slender fingers released the fabric. "Why are you shaking?"

She'd been wondering about that herself. Ever since she'd thought he was going to kiss her, she'd felt a little edgy. Maybe she was developing some exotic nervous disorder. "Just need a cup of coffee, I guess."

She didn't quite buy her own explanation, but apparently he did. "Sounds good. I could use some myself. Bring—"

"I'm not running a hotel," she cut in, certain he was about to tell her to bring him a cup. She'd planned on doing that anyway, but not until after she'd changed her clothes and checked on Craig.

The heavy slash of his dark eyebrows arched quizzically. "I was going to ask you to bring me my jeans so I could put the pot on while you take care of your patient. Be nice to me and I'll even bring you a cup."

It made no sense at all, but she had the craziest urge to throw the clothes bundled in her arms at his calm and very reasonable expression.

"You shouldn't get up," she advised him with a composure she didn't quite feel. "I'll go and see Craig and take care of the coffee in a few minutes."

She barely caught the smile he could no longer suppress when she turned and heard him call, "You do that," just before she closed herself in the bathroom.

A silent admonition that Nick's teasing didn't bother her in the least was followed by two deep breaths—and a longing glance cast in the direction of the narrow shower stall.

Her shower would have to wait. She was out of hot water, and the tepid stuff left in the little holding tank was all she had to wash up with. Sometime today she'd have to change propane tanks.

Quickly changing her clothes, she brushed her hair in its usual part down the middle and tied it behind her neck. It was a style she'd adopted for its efficiency but one that accentuated the startling darkness of her eyes and the almost too-sensual fullness of her mouth. The contrast of her black hair and heavy lashes against her smooth ivory skin lent a certain seductiveness to the vulnerability she could never quite erase from her eyes. Though, she supposed, stepping back from the yellowed mirror over the sink, the thick coat of mascara she'd just applied had helped a little. The gloss of lip balm she'd put on her mouth hadn't done a darn thing.

Smoothing the hem of her navy sweater over her hips—the form-fitting jeans she was wearing would have doubled the number of young male interns who used to follow her on her rounds—she stepped out into the hall.

The wonderful aroma of percolating coffee filled the air. It felt warmer, too. Nick had obviously put the coffee on, after all, and added the log to the stove. He was supposed to stay in bed and rest!

Refusing to engage in a battle of wills, she headed into the storage room. Short of tying Nick in bed, there was no way she could keep him there. At least Craig couldn't go anyplace.

"How does your leg feel this morning?" Her glance darted from the disapproval in Craig's sharp, ruddy features to Nick's scowl.

If the unfriendly glances the two men were bestowing on each other was any indication, it seemed she'd just interrupted some kind of disagreement. But Craig immediately replaced his displeasure with an affable smile when he looked over at her. The way his smile stretched wider as she moved to the cot made up for the deepening of Nick's frown.

"Throbbing like crazy," he replied, and nodded his gray head toward his elevated leg. "That's quite a contraption you rigged up there. I didn't get a chance to thank you for everything, or really introduce myself.'' He extended his hand. "Dr. Craig Williams," he offered, all but crushing her fingers in his grip. "I've been with Nick's team..."

Flexing her nearly mangled fingers, she listened as Craig continued and quickly checked his toes for swelling, then loosened a couple of the cloth strips she'd tied around the boards. Her task and Craig's dialogue—he was a medical doctor who'd joined Nick's team last year to conduct some behavioral research—made it a little easier to ignore the man sitting on the box at the foot of the cot.

Nick was dressed in his boots, jeans and the red-and-black flannel shirt he hadn't bothered to button. Between his brooding expression and the shadowy growth covering his clenched jaw, he looked quite... uncivilized.

What on earth is going on, she wondered, seeing the look of reproach Craig slanted at Nick.

Nick didn't catch it. He was too busy glaring at Tory.

Something Craig had said about the study he was conducting had piqued her interest. She wanted to ask him to tell her more about it, but the inexplicable tension filling the room made her change her mind in a hurry. There were more urgent matters to attend to, anyway.

Crossing her arms, she stepped back from the cot. "You shouldn't put any weight on that leg, Craig, so you'd better have Nick help you into the bathroom."

"We'll manage," Craig assured her, then arched a graying eyebrow in Nick's direction.

The men just looked at each other for a moment before Nick shook his head as if to say no.

Unable to interpret their silent exchange—Nick wasn't declining to help his friend, was he—she started out the door. They could work out the details. "I'll make us some breakfast."

Apparently the men didn't realize how thin the interior walls were. Even standing in the middle of the kitchen, she couldn't help but overhear their quiet conversation.

"What's eating you?" she heard Craig ask. "Don't you think she'll do it?"

"Keep your voice down." The admonishment was reinforced by the way Nick's voice lowered even more. "I don't plan on asking her."

Tory canceled the step she'd started to take, almost losing her balance as her head inched toward those voices. The men couldn't see her, but she could hear every word.

Craig had dutifully matched Nick's tone. "If everything checks out, why not?"

"Because I'm not sure I like the idea of having her—of having a woman around."

Maddeningly enough, Craig's voice dropped another notch.

"Female or not, I think she's got what it takes. She'd have to be strong to take on the job she's taken here, and she seems like the type who gets along with everybody."

"That isn't the point."

"Then would you mind telling me what is? Until I suggested this, you seemed to think she was . . ."

Craig's voice was so faint that just the sound of the log breaking apart in the stove made it impossible to discern the rest of his words. She didn't hear Nick's muttered response either, though it certainly wasn't for lack of trying.

Feeling a little cheated at not being able to hear the conclusion of that mysterious conversation, she filled a pot with water, dumped in some oatmeal and put it on the stove to boil.

A vague sense of unease joined her curiosity as she hunched down by one of the lower cabinets for the lid to the pot. Craig had said something about her being strong; reason told her he wasn't talking about physical strength. With a crew of supposedly able-bodied men, what use would her hundred and ten pounds be to them? He'd been talking about inner strength. The strength that, for Tory, had been born of denial.

She had no sooner entered her internship when Keith Richards, her husband of less than a month and the head of the surgical department she'd been assigned to, began the barrage of criticism that had eventually destroyed their marriage. He'd told her she'd never make it as a doctor; she wasn't tough enough. The emotional attachment she'd invariably developed with her patients had been viewed as a weakness. Their pain had been her pain. When someone died, she'd grieved. When a patient recovered, she'd walked on air for days.

She hadn't been the only intern with that problem. Several others had washed out that first year, unable to cope with the intensity of their feelings. But not Tory. Determined to prove to herself that she could make it, she'd discovered the secret to professional survival. She simply repressed emotion.

Outwardly, she did just fine. She could even hide the little things like irritation, pleasure, attraction and disquiet. No one ever saw the hurt or the joy she forced herself to deny. They caught glimpses of those feelings in the soft warmth of her eyes, but their depth was known only in that part of her soul she kept carefully locked away.

The fact that something about Nick was making it hard to keep a few of those minor feelings in check was a little disconcerting.

So were the sounds coming from around the corner.

It was amidst a considerable amount of swearing that she heard the bathroom door open and Nick and Craig weave back down the short hall.

"Ouch! Not that shoulder! Put your arm over here." That was obviously Nick.

"Sorry. But if you didn't take such big steps—"

"I'm not a pack mule, Williams."

"Well, this damn thing's heavy!"

Thump!

Tory grimaced. She hoped that whatever it was that had hit the wall wasn't Craig's leg.

Apparently it wasn't.

"You trying to get me into one of those things, too?"

"Cripes, Spencer," she heard Craig mutter. "We've been over mountains and glacier faces and down thousand-foot ravines. But I swear I never had any idea you were this clumsy."

Nick's grumbled reply contained an astonishing variety of expletives.

Tory might have been amused at their uncoordinated efforts, but she was too busy telling herself that the slight case of emotional vertigo she seemed to be suffering was only the result of all the changes she'd subjected herself to so recently. Nick had nothing to do with it. She wasn't attracted to him in the least.

No, she mentally corrected. She hadn't meant "attracted," she'd meant disturbed. Attraction implied something physical.

So what do you call what happened to you while you were lying in his arms, she prodded herself, and took a can of fruit from the cabinet. That, she continued, was nothing more than a normal female response to a...okay, an *attractive* male. Strictly a biological reaction.

She'd almost convinced herself that what she'd felt was nothing more than the product of starved nerve endings when she turned to find him standing behind her. How could a man look so appealing with a day's growth of scratchy beard?

"Give me the cups." His command was issued in the same uncompromising tone he'd used yesterday to order her back to the village. Tory hadn't like his tone then and liked it even less now.

Rather than trust herself to say anything, she reached into an overhead cupboard. An instant later, she felt his length pressing to her back. The sleeve of his shirt brushed her cheek when he reached past her, that spicy-musk scent she'd awakened to filling her nostrils. Her heart seemed to skip a couple of necessary beats when he leaned a little closer and extracted three bright yellow mugs.

"If you'll wait just a minute, I'll—"

Nick didn't wait for her to finish. Already he had moved to the counter and picked up the coffeepot.

She was trying very hard not to identify the feeling tightening her whole body when he motioned toward the pot on the stove.

"Is that all you've got?" He scowled at the thickly bubbling oatmeal.

Reaching behind her, she plunked the can of peaches down next to the cups. "And these. I'm sorry if it doesn't meet with your approval."

"I guess I don't have much choice," he replied dryly. "This'll do."

This'll do! Knowing if she were to stand there for another second he'd undoubtedly see the irritation she'd just put a name to, she grabbed the bowls from the shelf. She took a deep breath and allowed them to land unscathed on the counter.

"Here." He pushed one of the filled cups toward her, then glanced back at the unappetizing gruel in the pot. "You want me to dish that up for Craig, or are you going to wait until it develops a crust?"

Turning around so he couldn't see how white her knuckles were as she applied the can opener to the can of peaches, she muttered, "I thought I'd wait until the lumps dissolve. If you'll take Craig his coffee, I'll bring his breakfast in a minute."

Despite Craig's invitation for her to join him and Nick in the storage room for the meal *he* so clearly appreciated, Tory found herself sitting alone at the counter nursing her second cup of coffee. Craig had seemed to want her company, but Nick's cool glare told her he certainly didn't. Besides, she felt safer out here, away from the man whose presence was causing all sorts of problems with her heart rate and blood pressure.

She felt even safer when she went outside a few minutes later. The chore she was trying to tackle helped keep her from wondering how a man could wake up in a relatively pleasant mood, then abruptly turn into such a grouch.

Albert had told her how to change the propane tanks. At the time it hadn't sounded particularly difficult. However, theory and practice sometimes had little to do with each other. The mechanics she could handle; what she needed was some muscle. The full tank felt as though it weighed a ton. How was she ever going to lift it to the concrete slab next to the cabin without giving herself a hernia?

Each exerted breath was expelled in a puff of white vapor. She wasn't cold, with her heavy clothing and thick gloves, but she wasn't exactly warm, either. At least it wasn't snowing.

The tank was halfway between her cabinet and the combination wood-and-storage shed, when six barking malamutes announced Willy's arrival. Thank God, she sighed, smiling at the young boy's exuberant wave. Maybe he could help her with the cumbersome chore.

"Dad's called the coast guard," Willy puffed, adding his weight to hers while they slid the new tank into position. "He said to tell you and Dr. Spencer they'd be here in a couple of hours."

She wondered if there was any chance they'd take Nick back with them. "That's good, Willy. Can you hold this while I put the gauge back on? Tell me if I'm doing it right, okay?" She handed him the wrench.

Pleased with the duty she'd just assigned him, he carefully watched what she was doing. "If you need anything from Dutch, Dad's going over. The weather should stay clear now, so it's safe to make the trip."

Willy sounded so mature for his eleven years. Unlike their peers in the city, Aleut children seemed so capable, so levelheaded. They played just like other kids, but maybe their inborn respect for the vagaries of nature had something to do with their attitude.

"I don't need anything right now," she replied to Willy's offer. "But will you let me know the next time he goes over?"

The nearest market was in Dutch Harbor, which was on the northeastern side of the island. It was an all-day trip over and back.

Willy's response was as guileless as the boy himself. "Sure will. Dad says we've got to help you 'cause you don't have a man or nothing. And I'll help you 'cause you saved Tasha's puppies." Bright ebony eyes sparkled up at her. "Kai's getting real strong."

There was no way he could have known the relief behind her soft smile. Tory knew nothing about veterinary science. It had been only a heavy dose of blind luck that had enabled her to save the malamute's litter. Kai was the runt and Willy's favorite.

It wasn't talk of the puppy that caused his cherubic face to light in a wide grin—or Tory's mouth to compress. It was the sight of Nick, looking as glumly resigned as a patient facing necessary major surgery, coming around the side of the cabin to stop in front of them.

"Hi, Dr. Spencer!" Willy chirped to the man dwarfing his small frame.

Nick's features softened the instant he pulled his eyes from Tory and smiled affectionately at the beaming child. "Hi, yourself, sport. Got any messages for me?"

Nick hunched down, bringing himself eye level with Willy, who was repeating the information he'd given Tory. Tory, a bit more anxious than she cared to admit, turned away. Closing the latch on the woodshed, she tossed him a surreptitious glance.

The breeze was lifting the golden-brown strands of his casually styled hair. That same breeze seemed to carry the deep resonance of his voice swirling around her. But she wasn't hearing the words so much as she was feeling the effects of that slumberous voice.

You're losing it, Tory, she chided herself. Voices don't affect people that way! Think about something else. Like where you're going to put your garden when all this snow melts.

That's what she was doing a minute later when Nick, ruffling Willy's hair before sending him off with a manly slap on the back, stepped beside her.

Without the smile he'd given Willy, his mouth looked hard. And his eyes... Tory glanced away as quickly as she'd faced him. Those eyes could melt the North Pole or freeze the equator.

"Would you mind coming back in?" he asked, his tone as guarded as her expression. "Craig wants to see you."

She didn't want to go back inside, but she didn't think that trying to figure out where she was going to build the cold frame for the vegetables she wanted to try to grow was a good enough excuse to refuse his request. Why should she refuse anyway? It was Craig who wanted to see her.

Or so Nick had said.

No sooner had she dropped her jacket on the peg by the door and started toward the hall than Nick snagged her arm. "Just a minute," he said with a frown, and, dropping his hand, added his jacket to the row of pegs.

She matched his expression perfectly. "You said Craig—"

"I know what I said." He motioned toward the stools at the counter. "But I want to talk to you first."

He meant for her to sit down, but instead Tory leaned against the counter next to the closest stool. "Well?" she prompted when several seconds had passed and he hadn't said anything.

A muscle on his jaw jumped. "I can't talk to you when you're like that."

"Like what?"

"Like *that*. You've got defense written all over you. Look at the way you're holding your arms."

They were crossed protectively against her sweater. With a conscious effort, she dropped her hands to her sides. Now what should she do with them? The way they were just hanging there felt unnatural.

"That's better."

"Thanks."

"Look." The sigh in his voice was quite audible. "I don't know what your problem is, but I'd appreciate it if you'd settle down long enough to answer a few questions."

"What kind of questions? And what do you mean by 'settle down'?"

Until roughly fifteen hours ago, she'd been the epitome of outward calm. Maybe she'd lost a tiny bit of her practiced composure a couple of times, but certainly not enough to warrant his comment.

Nick seemed to think otherwise. "I mean just that. And you're doing it again."

"What am I doing?" Not even realizing it, her arms had resumed their former position.

"Damn it, Tory!"

It was the first time he'd called her by name. And she didn't appreciate its being preceded by an expletive. There was no doubt in her mind that he was trying to control his irritation with her, but she couldn't begin to imagine what she'd done to warrant it. "Six, seven, eight..." she muttered under her breath.

The network of tiny lines deepened around his narrowed eyes. "What are you doing?"

"Counting."

Though he was trying to maintain his implacable expression, his lips twitched upward at the corners. The hardness slipped from his eyes, gentling them to a pale aquamarine. "Do I make you that mad?"

"Possibly."

He seemed oddly pleased with that. The way his gaze flicked over her, then moved up slowly to settle on her mouth was more telling than the taunt in his words. "If I tell you why, you'd probably just deny it."

There had been something electric in the way he'd been looking at her mouth, and something quite knowing in his veiled half smile. She'd be willing to bet her stethoscope—if she had one here—that he thought she was piqued because he hadn't followed through with the kiss she'd expected this morning. The ego of the man was astounding. So was the fact that he just might be right.

She slid onto the stool. No sense standing there when her legs felt so unstable. "What do you want to talk to me about?"

The change of subject was glaringly obvious. But Nick didn't seem particularly interested in pursuing the matter she'd so hastily dropped. He turned around and jammed his hands into his pockets, which stretched the snug denim even tighter over his narrow hips. Tory moved her eyes to the middle of his broad back.

"First of all," he began in a tone as clipped as the strides he paced between her and the sofa, "you might as well know right now that I'm not crazy about this idea."

That disclaimer delivered, he turned to see what kind of reaction it provoked. Her expression was calmly expectant, but all he seemed to notice was that her arms were crossed again.

Rather than calling attention to it, he simply scowled and resumed his pacing. "Craig thinks you can help us—" that oddly resigned look she'd seen when he'd come outside was back "—and I'm afraid he's right. I don't see any other alternative."

Three

Nick had a definite knack for putting a person on the defensive. All Tory allowed to show, though, was her curiosity. Now she'd find out what he and Craig had been talking about earlier. "Just what is it you want?" she inquired, looking at him with an admirably disinterested gaze.

She'd seen his puzzlement over her controlled reactions a couple of times before. That look—as if he couldn't quite figure her out—lasted only long enough for him to pull out the stool next to her and, sitting down, plant his feet on the rungs. "I assume Albert told you what we're doing here?"

"Other than using the beach for an airstrip, you mean?"

The sardonic set of his mouth indicated that he wasn't interested in anything but direct answers.

"He said something about energy and earth-quakes," she amended with a shrug.

"Close enough. I think there's enough untapped energy under this chain of islands to ease up our dependence on oil and coal. Government and private industry are funding the expedition."

Tory remained silent while Nick explained what he and his crew would be doing and the problem he had encountered because of yesterday's accident. She couldn't help but admire the dedication and pride evident in his silky-rough voice. But it was only by forcing herself to concentrate on what he was saying, rather than on the beautiful mouth forming those words, that she was able to absorb the impact of his request.

There was no way she could hide her incredulity when he finally finished a few minutes later. She stared at him in unmasked disbelief. "You mean you want to move eight men in here and have *me* be camp doctor?"

He might not have been too happy with the idea himself, but he didn't look too pleased with having his proposal met with such an unencouraging reception, either.

"I said we'd bring in additional housing," he reiterated, trying to strengthen his case. "None of us would be in your way. We'd set the tents up on the other side of that rise out there and you wouldn't even see them."

"I thought you were setting your base up on Umnak."

"We were. But you're not over there." It was apparent that Nick didn't like having to repeat himself—and equally apparent he was prepared to do just that. "I told you, besides the research Craig's doing, he's also responsible for the men's medical needs. It doesn't matter where we put the base, here or on Umnak. What matters is that you've got a skill we need, and with Craig laid up...".

Nick paused and Tory took advantage of the momentary lull. "For someone who doesn't want me around, you sure are pushing the job."

He seemed to consider her observation while his glance darted from the slightly defiant tilt of her head to her knees, not missing a thing in between. "My reason for not wanting you around isn't as important as having access to your medical expertise. The men come first."

It was either the boldness of his quick, assessing appraisal or the honey coating the resignation in his tone that caused her to shiver. On the other hand, it could have just been the heat coming from the stove.

"What's that reason?" she returned, certain she already knew. She'd heard him tell Craig that having a woman around was a lousy idea—not in so many words, but that was the gist of it. He probably thought a woman around an all-male crew would cause trouble, but she was prepared to tell him she was quite capable of dealing with that kind of situation. She worked with men all the time. Gathering her defenses made her forget to ask herself if she even wanted the job in the first place.

The response she expected from Nick was not the one she got.

"My reason?" he repeated. When she nodded, he stared down at the worn spot on the knee of his jeans. "Let's just say that if I'd known we'd be here for longer than a day or two, I wouldn't have acted the way I did.''

"Like King Kong, you mean?"

The amused chuckle coming from the storage room reminded them of the man who could quite clearly hear their conversation.

"That's not what I mean and you know it," Nick mumbled in a dry half whisper and slid from his stool to stand in front of her. His voice lowered even more. "I'm talking about before breakfast and . . . well . . ." Drawing his hand through his hair he completed his explanation by muttering, "You know damn well what I'm talking about."

When he put it like that, she did. He was referring to the pass he'd made and the not-so-subtle game of tease and bait he'd been playing earlier. If he was seeking confirmation of that in her expression, he didn't get it. But he couldn't see the way her throat was tightening, either.

"If I've been less than friendly this morning," he continued tightly, "I apologize. Even if it is partly your fault."

"My fault? What did I do?"

One corner of his mouth lifted. "Nothing."

Uncomprehending sable eyes slanted up to meet a disquieting amount of self-directed reproach. "So what's the problem?"

"My curiosity."

"I'm obviously missing the point," she stated quietly, and pulled her knee back when his thigh brushed against it. Her skin beneath the denim tingled. "How can your curiosity and my doing nothing have anything to do with the way you've been acting?" At some point the conversation had slid from her grasp, and seemed to be taking on a life of its own.

"Maybe you'd understand if you knew what I was curious about."

"That might help," she conceded, wondering at the indecision playing over his rugged features. Did she really want to hear his answer?

He hesitated, but only briefly. "There's something I've wanted to do ever since you asked me if I was the idiot flying that plane. But I don't think it would be a very good idea if I want you to agree to take care of my men."

The dark wings of her eyebrows shot together. What was he curious about anyway? What it would feel like to strangle her? That certainly *wouldn't* be a very good idea. If he did, she wouldn't be around to take care of his crew.

"Well?" she prompted, knowing she wasn't in any mortal danger.

"You sure you want to know?"

At her affirmative nod, he leaned forward, trapping her between his arms by flattening his hands on the counter behind her. "I want to know what it would feel like to kiss you."

Only his arms were touching her. The rest of him was more than a foot away. "You had your chance," she informed him evenly. "But you blew it."

Mentally, her mouth flew open. Physically, she clamped it shut. She couldn't believe she'd said that!

Satisfaction flashed in turquoise eyes that had gone alarmingly dark. "You don't believe in second chances?"

Either he'd lowered his voice so it was impossible for Craig to hear, or the rushing in her ears had made his words barely audible. "I just don't think it'd be a very good idea." She repeated his earlier observation in a decidedly strained whisper.

"Neither do I," he agreed, and refuted that conviction by inching his head forward to brush his mouth against hers.

It began as nothing more than a light, almost impersonal touch designed to prove there was nothing special about the mouth he'd wanted to kiss. Tory allowed him that only because she'd wondered what it would feel like to kiss him, too. But what started as something almost clinical quickly changed to something far more sensual and much more intense.

Her lips parted with his gentle persuasion, his tongue slipping over her own as he drew her against him. The friction of his hand sliding up her back when he lifted her from the stool sent a frisson of tremors tracing that same path downward. The shudder racing the length of Nick's body only compounded that enervating phenomenon and she found herself clinging to him, as if his solid frame was the only stable thing in a world that had swung oddly out of kilter.

Nick must have felt that same dizzying sensation. When the pressure of his mouth lightened and he finally broke that drugging contact, he looked as shaken as she felt.

Drawing his hands to her shoulders, he eased her back down on the stool. He stepped back, clearing his throat. "I guess I shouldn't have done that," he said, running one finger over his eyebrow, then walked down the hall.

"Well?" she heard Craig ask. "Is she going to do it? You two got so quiet that I couldn't hear."

Nick's muttered "She didn't say" filtered toward her just before she heard him close the storage-room door.

Tory sank against the counter, her fingers pressed to her lips. Even now she could feel where his hands had flattened on her back, urging her against him, and the tender seduction that had been in his kiss.

She hadn't given him an answer because she hadn't had time to think about what Nick wanted her to do. And her thinking processes were suffering a major malfunction at the moment. All she could consider was how bewildered she was. There was something about Nick that made her feel things she hadn't felt in a very long time.

Tory hadn't realized how many bricks there were in the emotional wall she'd so carefully constructed. At least, she hadn't until Nick had started chipping away at them.

The Coast Guard helicopter transporting Craig was only a tiny silver speck in the only patch of blue sky. Slate-gray clouds had lost their identities as they merged into an even grayer shroud.

Nick pulled the collar of his heavy Sherpa jacket up behind his neck, his eyes fixed on the disappearing craft. "I'll need to radio over to Kodiak and let my men know what's going on."

Tory knew what he was getting at. He wanted to know if he should have them go over to Umnak Island and start setting up their base or come here. She replied quietly, "I'm still thinking about it," and rubbed her nose with the back of her gloved hand.

"Tory, we—"

"Nick, I—"

"You first," he offered, using the same guarded tone he'd employed since their little encounter several hours ago.

"No. You go ahead." Tory, too, had been careful to maintain her reserve.

Beneath his thick jacket, his chest expand with an indrawn breath. He exhaled slowly, the white vapor of his breath carried off by the cold breeze. The effort he was making to curb his impatience couldn't have been more obvious. Restraint marked his tone. "How much longer do you think you'll need before you decide?"

Ignoring his question, she chose to clarify what she and Craig had discussed. "Craig said you wouldn't need me while everyone's away."

"That's right. We'll be gone for a couple of weeks at a time, but you'd be here in case we had an emergency."

"And you won't expect me to do anything except take care of any of the men who get sick or hurt?"

The cleft in his chin seemed more pronounced when his jaw tightened. "Absolutely nothing."

She'd been having visions of turning into a sort of nursemaid for the crew—something she had no intention of doing, since her reason for being here was to take care of the people from the village. Craig had assured her that her only duties would be medical ones, but she'd wanted to hear it from Nick.

Barely meeting the eyes that were barely meeting hers, she shrugged. "If you can get me the things I need, I guess it'll be all right."

Nick had already said he would. In return for her agreement, he'd offered to replace the medical supplies she'd told him were in storage. Having no idea

how long it would take to untangle that mess with the movers, his offer had seemed quite acceptable.

If Nick was pleased with her decision, he was doing a remarkable job of keeping it to himself. "Fine," he pronounced quietly. "Go make a list of what you want. I'm going to Albert's to use the radio." He took one step away, then stopped and turned around. "Thanks, Tory." He almost smiled before hunching his shoulders and heading toward the cluster of weather-beaten cabins forming the heart of the village a quarter mile away.

Nick had been gone for nearly four hours. Thankful for her assigned task, and his absence, Tory finally produced a satisfactory list of supplies, drugs and equipment. Craig had seemed to think that all she'd be doing for the crew was treating cuts, scrapes and an occasional cold. "If you can stitch them up here," he'd said, "it would sure be more convenient than having to haul someone three hundred miles to the naval station at Adak or six hundred the other way to Kodiak."

Just how clumsy were these people anyway, she wondered, tapping her pen on the arm of the sofa.

Casting materials were added to her list.

Tucking her feet beneath her, she again checked everything she'd written down. Every item had been all but memorized and it was pointless going over it again. Knowing she was only trying to keep her mind occupied, and realizing the futility of it, she laid the list on the cushion beside her. Now what?

She supposed she could read. Besides all the novels she'd brought with her, there was plenty of reading material under her bed. Or she could write another

letter to her folks. Or she could get the instruction book and see if she could figure out how to play her balalaika. But any one of those things would take either patience or concentration, neither of which she felt capable of at the moment.

Where was he? If he hadn't planned on coming back to her cabin tonight, he could at least have had the decency to let her know. It was impossible for him to call—there were no telephones in the village, the only form of communication with the rest of the world being Albert's radio—but Nick could have sent a message through Willy.

If Nick made her feel anything at all, it was plain old irritation.

It had been raining for quite a while. The wind seemed to be blowing harder now, carrying the sheeting drops at sharp angles against the windows. Rather than sitting here doing nothing, she'd better go and close the shutters.

Telling herself she should just be grateful he'd chosen to stay away, she sat at the foot of her bed pulling on her boots. Then she glanced past the beige curtains next to her and saw him disappearing behind the woodshed. Her fingers seemed to tangle in her laces. A moment later she heard the door open, then close again. It didn't sound as though Nick had come in.

It wasn't until she nearly tripped over it that she noticed the knapsack lying by the front door. A second later, she heard the distinct sound of wooden shutters being slammed together. The shutters in the living room were already closed. Nick must have been working his way around the cabin. Sure enough, a moment later a loud thump came from the general direction of her room.

You're not nervous, she lied to herself, waiting until she heard his feet hit the step outside. Then, wiping her damp palms on her jeans, she pulled the door open.

"I hope you don't mind," he began, stepping from the rapidly dimming daylight into the cozy warmth of the room, "but I'll have to stay here until the crew arrives with the tents. Albert offered me Anton's half of Willy's bed, but I'm afraid I might roll over on a puppy." He paused, then added, "I'll sleep in the storage room."

His tone was so polite it sounded stiff. Tory matched it perfectly. "I don't suppose it makes any sense for you to stay anywhere else, since you'd just be coming back here anyway. I'll put some clean sheets on the cot."

"Don't bother. I brought a sleeping bag." He shrugged out of his wet jacket and handed it to her. "I couldn't find a latch on the woodshed, so I propped a piece of driftwood in front of the door to keep the wood dry."

Her mumbled "Thank you" was directed to his jacket. Though the outside fabric was cold and damp, the soft lining still held the warmth of his body.

A pair of sealskin pants stretched over Nick's jeans. Many of the men in the village wore them because the waterproof hide provided both protection from dampness and insulation from the cold. She figured Albert must have lent them to him as Nick leaned against the wall and pulled off his boots. The outer pair of pants came next.

Tory glanced away. When he bent over like that the way his jeans molded his muscled thighs and tight buttocks seemed almost indecent.

Droplets of water pelted the wall when she gave his jacket a decisive shake and dropped it on the hook next to hers. "Are your men coming tomorrow?" she inquired politely.

Nick carried his wet boots to the stove. "I don't know."

"I thought you were going to use the radio to call them."

"I used the radio to check you out. I'll talk to my men in the morning."

His implacable gaze told her he was expecting something other than her quietly spoken "Oh."

The way his thick eyebrows snapped together seemed to question her reaction—or, rather, her lack of one. There was no reason for her to question what he'd done, though. He had a perfect right to know if the doctor who would be caring for his men was qualified. She wasn't going to ask for confirmation, but she was certain anything he'd learned had been favorable.

"Is your list ready?" Apparently Nick felt his inquiry was confirmation enough.

Retrieving it from the sofa, she handed it to him. It was a toss-up as to who pulled back more quickly when her fingers inadvertently brushed his. Tory stepped a little farther away.

For a moment they just stood there, hooded aquamarine eyes meeting guarded brown ones. Neither was going to drop the wall of caution. Yet, even as he carefully folded the paper and tucked it into the pocket of his jeans, his eyes never left her face.

Tory had never thought of air having any consistency, but suddenly it felt so thick she could barely breathe. In a voice so strained it didn't even sound like her own, she asked, "Have you eaten yet?"

"I had lunch at Albert's."

Did that mean he didn't want dinner? "There's a stew here if you're hungry."

"Thanks. I'll see that any of your provisions I use are replaced."

That wasn't necessary, but all she could say was, "Fine."

She couldn't stand it anymore. She had to look somewhere—anywhere—rather than at him. The room was filling with a tension almost overpowering in its intensity. Had it been dark, she was certain that jagged yellow bolts of electricity could have been seen bouncing off the walls.

Turning away, she focused on the window over the sink. The wind leaking around the frame ruffled the heavy blue curtains.

When Nick finally picked up his knapsack and took it into the storage room, Tory let out an audible sigh. It felt as though she'd been holding that breath for the last five minutes.

Two bowls of canned stew sat cooling on the counter. Tory's appetite had deserted her. Maybe she'd never have one again. The knot in her stomach felt permanent.

Nick sat at the opposite end of the counter, a short five feet away, picking at his meal. The strain was definitely beginning to get to her. They hadn't said a word to each other in the last twenty minutes. For no other reason than she knew she'd go crazy if one of them didn't say something soon, she pushed her bowl aside and asked the most innocuous thing she could think of. "Has your shoulder bothered you today?"

"A little," he replied, playing with a piece of potato. "You sure I didn't crack something?"

She hadn't expected anything more than a flat "No." Her eyes darted toward him. "I don't think so. But without an X ray it's impossible to tell for sure."

Was he going to ask her to look at it again? She didn't think her nerves would survive if she had to touch him. To avoid the possibility of that request, she opted for a verbal means of diagnosis. "I said you should be keeping it relatively immobile. You weren't using it today, were you?"

"Maybe a little." He was still talking to his stew. "I helped Albert chop firewood while I was waiting for some of my calls to be returned."

If he'd done something that stupid, he deserved to have it hurt. "I'm not surprised it's bothering you then." Since he was directing his half of this conversation to his bowl, she pulled her glance back to the counter.

A moment later, she felt rather than saw his eyes on her. Instead of looking up, she continued to study the Formica, her fingernail tracing a tiny, meandering crack. Salmon pink had never been her favorite color.

"You think you should tape it or something?" he asked.

"Taping won't do any good if you're going to use it anyway."

"What if I don't use it?"

"Then it doesn't need to be taped."

Again, silence filled the room. Maybe she should take a look at his shoulder. If she could see it only as a *pectoralis major* joined to a clavicle, she should be able to handle it.

Taking a deep breath, she slid off the stool. "The light's better over here," she said, indicating the seat she'd just vacated.

As if there hadn't been a sixty-second gap in their conversation, Nick pulled off his sweater and moved over to sit in front of her. Carefully avoiding his eyes, she forced herself to see only the darkening bruise on his left shoulder. Her self-discipline was definitely being tested. She'd caught only a glimpse of the corded muscle and sinew rippling over his back, but the banded muscles of his chest with their mat of thick golden-brown hair seemed to be taunting her. How could she touch him with her hands shaking as they were?

Nick's feet were planted on the lower rung of the stool, his knees forming a wide V. She had to take a step closer if she was going to get a good look at the bruise, and that would mean stepping into the space between his denim-covered legs.

Keeping her eyes on his shoulder, she took that tentative step. "It isn't swollen," she noted as clinically as possible. "Give it a few days' rest and it should be all right."

"How long's a few?"

"Three or four."

He shook his head, his expression as cool and unrevealing as it had been all day. "I've got a camp to set up when my men get here."

"Then why ask for my advice if you don't have any intention of following it?"

"I didn't ask for your advice," he replied evenly. "I just asked if you thought it was only bruised or if something else was wrong."

Count to ten, Tory, she warned herself, and stepped away from the legs that were dangerously close to touching hers. No, better make that twenty. She wasn't going to be the first to put an end to the cold war by losing her temper. Temper? Until yesterday, she hadn't even known she'd had one.

Reaching for the heavy green sweater he'd laid on the counter, she very calmly handed it to him. "It's not that warm in here. Unless you want to catch cold, I suggest you put this back on. It's only a suggestion," she added. "Not advice."

The thick lashes surrounding his eyes narrowed as he studied her hard-won composure. That piercing gaze fell on her back when she picked up her untouched dinner and quietly announced, "I'm going to bed."

From the corner of her eye she saw him glance at his watch. "Do you always go to bed at seven o'clock?"

Was it only seven? "I'm going to read."

She scraped her dinner into a plastic container. Since food was not something to be wasted here, she'd reheat her portion for herself tomorrow.

The only sounds filling the room were the howl of the wind whipping rain against the cabin and Tory's deliberately quiet attempt to clean up the small kitchen. She was trying to minimize the noise of washing dishes because every sound seemed magnified by the increasingly unnerving silence.

The pot had just been dried and put away when Nick carried his bowl to the sink. "Do you want me to put more wood in the fire?"

Tory didn't even glance up from the stove as she wiped it off. "Please."

Something heavy slammed on the drain board, the sound angry and sharp. Whirling around, she saw Nick facing the sink, his broad back to her. He hadn't put his sweater back on and tension seemed to spring from the bands of muscle stretching inward to the long, smooth line of his spine. It was several very long seconds before he turned to face her.

"I want to ask you a favor," he stated in a tone much calmer than she'd expected. "Do you think we could call a truce?"

Carefully keeping the suspicion from her voice—and her eyes off that distracting, naked chest—she asked, "What's the favor?"

Nick's face was a study in stone. Hard planes and angles were held together by a look of seeming indifference. That look puzzled her—even more so when she saw the merest trace of a smile working at the corner of his mouth. From where she was standing she couldn't be sure that there wasn't the slightest light of a smile in his eyes, too.

The strangled grip she had on the dishcloth—she'd almost jumped out of her skin when she'd heard his fist hit the counter—eased a little.

"Do we have a truce?" he inquired.

"Temporary...or permanent?"

"Probably only temporary." He was smiling! Not much, but enough.

"How temporary?"

"Five minutes?"

Tory drew her bottom lip between her teeth, considering. "All right," she agreed. "Five minutes. What do you want?"

"A back rub."

"What?"

"You heard me. A back rub. My neck's killing me."

"I thought you said it was your shoulder that hurt."

"I lied." The smile turned to a full-blown grin revealing a row of even white teeth.

"And your neck is what made you so upset?" she asked, alluding to his behavior of a moment ago.

"No," he returned simply. "That was your fault."

The smile on Tory's lips vanished. If he wanted a truce, he certainly wasn't acting like it. "You've got four and a half minutes left." Her threat wasn't anywhere near as evident as she'd wanted it to be.

"Does that mean you'll do it?"

"Under one condition."

"Name it. I'm desperate."

How could she be indifferent to him when he looked so sincere? Indifferent? Nick made her feel a lot of things, but indifference wasn't one of them.

"Well?" he prompted, resuming his former position on her stool. "What's the condition?"

She moved to stand behind him. "I'll let you know if it comes up, okay?"

"Whatever you say. You're the doctor."

Bottom lip clamped between her teeth and taking a deep breath, Tory laid her hands on the smooth skin at the base of his neck. "Drop your head," she instructed.

He did. Seconds later, when her hands began their gentle kneading, he let out an audible sigh.

Okay, Tory, she began to herself, this is the trapezius and this is the deltoid. Her hands worked efficiently over the muscle running from his neck to his shoulder and then to the muscle at the back of his upper arm. And this is the *latissimus dorsi*, she reminded herself, feeling the pliant skin of his midback sliding beneath her fingers. Now the vertebrae. First the cervical—she rolled her thumbs down his neck, eliciting another deep, contented sigh—and then the thoracic. Her thumbs made little circles along either side of his spine as she worked her way down to his belt. Finishing that thorough manipulation, she started all over again—both the massage and her silent, technical dialogue.

She could feel him relaxing beneath her hands. But where the tension left his body, it seemed to be transferring itself to hers. No amount of mental gymnastics could make her deny how wonderful his skin felt or the crazy sensation flopping around in the pit of her stomach.

Tory withdrew her hands abruptly. "Your five minutes are up."

Nick turned around on the stool and hooked his hands around her waist. With a slight tug, he pulled her between the V of his legs. "I'd like to negotiate an extension of that truce."

"Not possible. You just breached the condition."

"You didn't tell me what the condition was, so how can I have breached it?" His chiding was gentle. So was the feel of his hands, though they tightened a little when she started to pull back. "What was it, anyway?"

"That you—" Her vocal cords seemed just as weak as her legs felt. Clearing her throat, she began again. "That you not touch me."

"That's hardly fair. You had your hands all over my back."

"That was different."

A lazy half smile teased the corner of his mouth. Tory wondered if he was even aware of what his hands were doing. They had spread out around her waist, his fingers absently working at the fabric. The man was a magician; his simplest touch turning her into a mindless mass of quivering nerves.

Arching her back away from him, she dropped her head and saw her stomach pressed to the edge of the stool. Nick shifted again.

The knot in her stomach coiled. The insides of his thighs now pushed against her hips. He'd just locked his feet behind her calves.

"I think you and I need to talk," he said quietly.

"Do we have to talk like this?"

"No. But I'd prefer it. This way I can see your eyes."

She didn't think that was such a great idea and immediately averted her gaze to his chest. That didn't seem to be a very safe place to look, either. Lowering them farther, she encountered the zipper of his jeans.

Some efforts at evasion are more trouble than they're worth, she thought, dropping her lashes so she couldn't see anything.

"Tory, come on." Lifting her chin with one finger, he coaxed her head back up. "The sooner we get this over with, the easier it'll be for both of us."

Four

Tory's arms crossed protectively over her sweater, her fingers biting into her upper arms when she pulled back—as far as she could, anyway. Nick had lowered his hands from her waist, but with his legs locked behind her, the distance between them was negligible at best.

Her skepticism was quite apparent as she tipped her head to one side. "Get what over with?"

"Take it easy," he soothed, eyeing her defensive stance with resignation. "I just want to ask a question."

"What kind of question?"

"A theoretical one."

Her fingers relaxed a little, restoring the circulation in her arms. That sounded safe enough.

"Have you ever found yourself in a situation," he began when her expression grew expectant, "where you knew the technical answers, but there was something that made you want to ignore them? Something that made you overlook everything you'd learned and want to question those answers?"

The delicate line of her eyebrows lowered. "Do you mean professionally?"

He nodded, watching her.

"I suppose so." She thought his question a little odd to require the intimacy of their positions. If they were going to talk theory, why couldn't they do it from opposite sides of the counter?

"What if you discover that the answers were right in the first place and you'd just wasted a lot of energy for nothing?"

"In that case," she assured him, "I'd know better next time."

"You wouldn't conduct the same experiment again?"

"There wouldn't be any reason to. If you know the results will be the same, it would be a waste of time."

His eyes remained steady on hers, something in those searching depths keeping the rather strange topic just the other side of neutral. Or maybe it was the pressure of his thighs against her hips that made what he was saying take on a less abstract meaning. "What if we were talking about personally instead of professionally? Your same answer still apply?"

"You're talking about two entirely different things," she returned without hesitation. "On a personal level you deal with people, not chemicals or known quantities. Too many variables."

"Exactly."

It was always nice to know you'd given the right answer. It would help enormously, though, if she'd understood the question. "Exactly what?"

A rueful smile touched his lips. Glancing at his hand resting on his thigh, he flexed his fingers. "You're an unknown quantity, Tory. The variable that could disprove the answer."

The hand he'd been studying lifted, suspending itself in midair before reaching over to trace the line of her jaw. His touch was so light, so electric that the nerves controlling her vocal cords seemed to short-circuit. Though she'd opened her mouth to ask for clarification of his puzzling analogy, no sound would come out.

"You're a very beautiful woman," he continued, carrying his touch to her neck, then up to the other side of her face. "You feel so soft." His fingers stilled when they reached her mouth. "And when your lips are parted like this, they invite a man to kiss them. But your eyes—" an indescribable softness crept over the shadowed angles of his face "—your eyes are the most haunting I've ever seen. Such intelligence, but so wistful. Almost . . . sad."

Within seconds, he'd made her forget to be wary. He was telling her he appreciated more than what was visible on the outside. Somehow he could see the woman that lay beneath the soft skin and inviting mouth. It was there in his eyes.

That realization should have frightened her. Surprisingly, it didn't. Even more astonishing was what she was feeling. For the first time in years, she had just allowed herself to acknowledge the depth of that often-denied sensation, the one that settled heavily in her chest like a weight pressing down on a void.

Loneliness.

What puzzled her was why she was feeling it now. Without knowing how, she knew Nick was feeling it, too. In his unguarded expression, she could see an empathy he had yet to verbalize. But the words weren't necessary. Even without them, she knew he was sharing something of himself he seldom let anyone see.

The void seemed to close a little. And when a gentle smile formed on his lips, something warm squeezed around her heart.

"It's not an easy thing to admit, is it, Tory? But it's something some of us have to learn to live with. I guess it's the price we pay for having what we want."

The telepathy passing between them was uncanny, his perception startling. Loneliness was the price she'd paid by denying the pain and pleasure of emotion, the price she'd had to pay to reach her goal.

"Is it worth it?" she ventured, hesitant.

He must have sensed that she'd asked the question of herself even as she posed it to him. "You'll have to answer that one for yourself, but for me…most of the time. My work is interesting, it's fulfilling a need, and it keeps me outdoors." That disarming little-boy smile curved his mouth. "I don't like confinement. Probably has something to do with being raised with five brothers in a three-bedroom house. Nobody ever had enough space." Despite his words, his smile widened, betraying a wealth of pleasant memories. Then it softened to something more pensive. "Even when I was teaching I couldn't wait for classes to be over so I could get out of the building."

His shift from the philosophical and abstract had been so rapid Tory scarcely had time to digest the information he was giving her. "You taught?"

The light caught the traces of gold threading through his hair when he nodded. "For four years. Geology and earth sciences."

"Why did you quit?"

"Too confining."

"Oh."

"What about you? Any brothers or sisters?"

There was one thing to be said for his conversational leaps. Trying to keep up with him made it easier to forget about the heat of his thighs burning against her. "None," she replied.

"Parents?"

"Two."

"Come on," he prodded, looking to see if that was a smile tugging at her lips. "Where are they? What do they do?"

"They live in San Diego. They're retired psychologists."

"That explains it."

"Explains what?"

"Why you seemed so interested when Craig was explaining his study to you before he left. Did you ever think of going into that field?"

"I thought about it. But I thought I could help in a different way, by being a doctor."

Why was she telling him this? Must have something to do with his eyes, she supposed. The CIA could have used them for interrogation purposes. They did seem to block out everything else and make it impossible not to answer.

Her head tilted to one side as she studied the man who held her captive. "What are you trying to do?"

He seemed to appreciate her skepticism. "I think I'm trying to get to know you, and give you a chance to get to know me. Isn't that all right?"

She wasn't sure.

"Don't do that." He frowned when she tried to move back, and the pressure of his hands bit into her waist. "It's time we started cooperating with each other, and pulling away won't help."

The feel of his hands elicited a heat that threatened to vaporize her body fluids. Apparently the moisture in her mouth had been the first to go. Her lips felt positively parched. "How do you propose we cooperate?"

An unexpected hint of mischief danced in his eyes. "The best way would probably be to take opposite corners and converse politely about our basic philosophies. But right now...." His hesitation seemed to stem more from some internal uncertainty than a pause for effect, and his voice grew huskier. "But right now, I'd like you to do this." He touched his fingers to her jaw, lightly tracing its shape, then moved them slowly over her mouth.

The faint noise in her ears could have been the sound of the rain pelting the roof...or the soft thud of a brick falling from her wall of protection. When he picked up her hand a moment later and pressed it to his jaw, she could only whisper, "Like this?" and let her fingers imitate his motions.

Nick appeared to concentrate on what she was doing, then nodded. "Now, you do this."

Shifting slightly, he scooted forward on the stool. Mere inches separated them now. His hands brushed over her shoulders and slid down her sides. Stopping there, his fingers splayed around her ribs, his thumbs resting just below the fullness of her breasts. Bending forward his lips grazed the smooth skin of her neck. Seconds later they found the warmth behind her ear, then began to travel along her throat. When his lips reached her chin, he continued the same journey along the other side, ending when he again returned to her neck.

The bones in her legs felt like damp sponge. Eyes closed against the exquisitely tender quest, she was conscious only of the breathtaking sensations his gentle touch evoked. Her dark lashes fluttered open when he drew his head away.

Nick was watching her quietly, his eyes bidding her to follow his actions.

Remembering every step he'd taken, Tory's fingers slid over his broad shoulders, feathering along the hard muscles of his sides. His skin looked like molten gold in the soft lamplight, and felt like warm velvet. Tentatively, she touched her lips to the base of his throat. His scent filled her lungs, increasing the rapid tempo of her heart. If a person was assigned only a certain number of heartbeats in a lifetime, Nick had just taken ten years away from her.

The flesh of his neck and the curve behind his ear felt smooth beneath her lips, the skin of his jaw with its night time stubble of new growth erotically rough. Certainly he must be able to feel her trembling. There wasn't a nerve in her body that wasn't responding to him.

Just as he had done, she took her time, then pulled her head away. Her dark eyes looked like pieces of shining ebony when she met the barely restrained desire in his.

"Now," he whispered, cupping her face, "we'll do something together."

Slowly, cautiously, he drew her face to his. Their lips touched lightly, the deliberate lack of urgency only increasing the sensual torture. Then the pressure increased and his mouth began to move with measured leisure. Her lips grew pliant against the quiet assault and they parted, allowing the unhurried intrusion of his tongue.

She didn't know which one of them deepened the kiss. It didn't matter. The warmth of his tongue caressed the smooth flesh inside her mouth, her own matching each thrust and parry. There were no demands. Each took only what was returned. It was nothing more than an unconcealed need to discover, nothing less than two souls reaching out in silent communication of a need neither was prepared to verbalize.

"Nick," she breathed, carrying her kiss across his cheek to his eyelids. It felt so natural to be touching him like this, so right to whisper his name.

He must have felt the rightness of it, too. Tangling his fingers through her hair, he guided her head to his shoulder. For nearly a minute he just held her, resting his chin on her head while he slowly stroked her back.

A tremulous sigh escaped her lips. She knew it was only a fleeting thing, a moment in time as fragile as a single snowflake losing itself among billions of others. Something that was, then wasn't. But no one had ever made her feel so protected before. So cherished. Certainly not Keith.

It had never occurred to her before that she and Keith had never made love. They'd only had sex. What Nick was doing now, simply by holding her, was making love.

"You know," Nick began when another minute had passed, "this kind of cooperation could get us both in trouble." Lifting her arms from his neck, he clasped her hands between his. "I told Craig I didn't want you around because I was afraid of the effect you'd have on the men—but it's the effect you've had on me I'm really worried about."

Most men wouldn't have confessed that kind of vulnerability. But Nick wasn't most men. There was something unique even about the way he delivered that matter-of-fact admission.

"If it makes you feel any better—" her hand drifted to the pulse beating at the base of his throat, and she found that his heartbeat was no calmer than hers "—I think I know what you mean."

She allowed her fingers to trace the chiseled angle of his jaw. The need to touch him was overwhelming. Almost as overwhelming as the feelings beginning to break free inside her.

What she couldn't understand was why she wasn't trying to push those feelings back. Nick wasn't the kind of man she needed. The existence he'd chosen for himself was a Gypsy's life, always moving from one isolated spot to the next. There was no room in that kind of life for a real relationship.

It's because this isn't really happening, she tried to rationalize. And if it isn't happening, it can't hurt me.

For what seemed like forever, he continued to hold her with the clear intensity of his eyes. Then, in a gesture that nearly turned her knees to water, he pressed a kiss into her palm.

"I've been thinking about it a lot today, Tory." He glanced up when her fingers curled and she slowly pulled her hand away. "The way I see it, we can either practice preventive medicine by avoiding each other, or..."

He let his words trail off, allowing what he was leaving unsaid to take its impact from silence. It was obvious enough what that *or* was.

Stepping out of his arms, she grabbed his sweater from the counter. She wasn't ready to make that kind of decision. It was too soon. Far too soon. "You'd better put this back on."

"Put that down and come back here."

She dropped the sweater but stayed right where she was—a nice, relatively safe six feet away.

It looked as though Nick was trying very hard not to smile. "I take it your not-so-subtle message is that you're going to stay out of my way?"

"You're the one who should stay out of mine," she returned, fighting the urge to back up another foot. She was usually quite good at holding her ground. "You were the one who came barging into my life. Remember?"

"I didn't come barging in," he corrected her smoothly. "I crashed."

Her muttered "You can say that again" earned her a complying shrug.

"Okay, I didn't come barging—"

"I didn't mean it literally," she all but groaned.

That tiny half smile of his was terribly unnerving—almost as disorienting as the sensations still lingering everywhere he'd touched her. Refusing to dwell on intangibles, she gave him an indulgent look. This topic was much easier to discuss than the one they'd just abandoned. "The point is that none of this was my idea. You're the one who wants to turn this place into Camp Catastrophe."

"You think that's what it's going to be?"

"Only when you're here." She smiled sweetly. "I'm sure everything'll be fine when you're out in the field."

He feigned a look of defeat. "I guess I'll have to make sure I only come back for provisions then."

That didn't sound like such a bad idea, but she could go him one better. "If you'd like, I could probably arrange to have them sent to you." She hadn't meant to sound quite so teasing. She was serious, darn it!

He stepped closer to pick up his sweater. "You probably could. On the other hand, you could bring them yourself." Lifting her chin with his finger, he added, "It's going to be a long year, Tory."

Before she could form a response—not that she had the slightest idea what to say to that incongruous statement—he'd turned and started down the hall. "Let's have something besides oatmeal in the morning," he called back. "I can't stand the stuff."

The storage-room door closed with a soft thud.

Tory leaned against the counter, pressing her hand to her head as if the motion could still the thoughts careening through her brain. Oddly enough, the only one that registered was so insignificant it wasn't worth dwelling on.

Nick had said something about preventive medicine. Didn't he know that kind of treatment worked only before a person contracted the disease?

Maybe that thought wasn't so insignificant after all. A simple attraction could be dealt with. It was the potential posed by that attraction that she needed to avoid. Sort of like the difference between mild heart palpitations and a coronary.

Nick didn't have oatmeal for breakfast the next morning—not unless someone in the village fed it to him. He was gone when Tory got up but would be returning shortly. Or so Katrina Nuclief had said when she'd arrived at Tory's cabin a couple of hours ago. Nick wouldn't be alone, though. Some of his men were arriving today after all.

Tory wasn't thinking about Nick or his crew at the moment. "Are you sure this'll taste okay?" She didn't mean to sound so doubtful, but she couldn't help it any more than she could help pulling her glance from Katrina to dubiously eye the contents of the Dutch oven on her stove.

Staring back at her was a chunk of sea lion swimming in a sea of broth and onions. The meat had been a gift from Katrina.

Subsistence living hadn't sounded all that unappealing, what with the sea yielding its bounty of halibut, crab, salmon and a myriad of other delicacies. Tory would take seafood over steak any day. But sea lion? She gave herself a mental pat on the back for having had the foresight to stock up on canned goods.

"It'll be wonderful," Katrina assured her. "When you had it at my house, you thought it tasted like beef."

Tory hadn't known what she was eating at the time. "And liver," she supplied. "Beef and calves' liver."

"Well, I've never tasted either one of those, so I'll just take your word for it. Shall we make the *aladika* now?"

Tory smiled at the woman who had so freely offered her friendship. Like many of the other older women in the village, the wrinkles in her face were etched deeply despite the plumpness of her cheeks. She wore her straight black hair loosely down her back, held by a whalebone comb. But when she smiled, all you could see was the inner contentment radiating from her beautiful black eyes, and the genuineness of the woman herself. It was hard not to envy her.

"The *aladika*," Tory repeated, returning her attention to her lesson in native cooking. "That's fried bread, isn't it?"

At Katrina's nod, Tory tried to hide her trepidation. As long as a meal came from a can or a box, she did just fine. Making something from scratch took a talent that seemed beyond her. "I'm willing if you are. You and Albert and Willy will have to stay for dinner, though. There'll be enough food here to feed an army."

The villagers were a very social people, and any excuse to get together with a neighbor was quickly acted upon. "We'd like that very much," Katrina replied, then surprised Tory by declining. "But you'll need everything you have for Dr. Spencer and his men. I'm sure they'll be starving by the time they finish setting up their tents." Tory's smile turned wry as the older woman continued, "Dr. Spencer will appreciate having a meal ready. Now, let's get everything out so all you have to do is mix the dough."

Tory dutifully produced the requested ingredients. She had the feeling Nick had recognized her lack of culinary skills, what with the lumpy oatmeal she'd prepared and the canned stew he'd barely touched. Obviously, sending Katrina over here had been a silent plea for gastronomic help.

Despite his earlier assurances, he expected her to feed him and his men—tonight, anyway. No wonder he'd sent Katrina to tell her his men were arriving instead of doing it himself. He knew Albert's wife wouldn't question the need to have a meal ready, but if he'd suggested it to Tory...

Her smile deepened. Beneath Nick's rugged exterior beat the heart of a chicken.

Katrina had asked for whale oil. Tory was trying to look apologetic for not having any—one foreign substance a day was about all she could handle—when the whir of helicopters sliced through the air. The deafening racket increased, then receded moments later, and the sound of male voices punched through the din.

"At the risk of sounding obvious," Tory remarked, wondering at the anticipation in her tone, "it seems Nick's men are here."

Both women hurried to the window, Tory gripping a handful of the heavy blue curtain. She wasn't quite sure why, but she was looking for Nick.

Within minutes the flurry of activity outside her pitch-roofed cabin had increased to storm-velocity proportions. A huge helicopter, its twin rotors now stilled, sat like a giant brown insect on the flat white plain. A smaller helicopter sat a little farther beyond. So many of the villagers had trudged over the hill to watch the excitement, some arriving by sled and on horseback, that it was impossible to tell how many of

Nick's men had arrived. There had to be close to forty people colorfully dotting the pristine landscape.

The bright yellows, reds and greens of the babushkas that many of the women wore on their heads, mingled with the deep purples and blues of the sheepherders' wool coats. Seal hunters and fishermen wandered about in their gray sealskin parkas. Even the Russian Orthodox priest was there, his long gray beard and black robes flapping in the wind. Teenagers were conspicuous only because there were so few of them. Most had been sent off to school in Anchorage or the lower states.

Crates were being hoisted to the ground, and a human chain formed to pass them to a metal shed that had been erected with surprising speed. Children were darting everywhere, the ones venturing toward the helicopters being shooed back by the nearest adult. In the middle of it all, Nick could be seen directing the chorus of organized confusion.

Tory and Katrina glanced at each other. With a simultaneous shrug, they grabbed their jackets and headed out the door. Katrina didn't want to miss what was going on; Tory told herself she just wanted to be sure they didn't erect a tent atop the ground she wanted to use for her garden. That probably wouldn't be a problem, though. Nick had promised he'd put the tents up where she wouldn't have to look at them.

Pulling her white stocking cap over her ears, Tory moved into the chattering crowd. Katrina had spotted her niece, a young woman of twenty who was almost five months pregnant, and the two of them had already disappeared. Tory had also lost sight of Nick.

"Dr. Richards?" A man in a navy-blue pea coat, his wiry brown hair curling around the edges of a blue knit cap, touched her arm. "You're the only one here who looks like the lady I'm looking for," he said, stepping in front of her. He thrust out his hand, a pleasant smile stretching over her freckled face. "You are Dr. Richards, aren't you?"

Returning his infectious smile, she pulled her gloveless hand from her pocket to accept his handshake. "I am. And you're . . . ?"

"Brian Godfrey. Physicist and soon to be resident expert on geothermal energy. Well, second expert behind our benevolent leader." Letting go of her hand, he rubbed his own hands together. "At the moment, though, I'm the flunky in charge of ground operations, which is one way of saying, 'Where don't you want our tents?'"

Instinctively she knew she was going to like this man. "Anywhere except over there." Her head dipped toward a patch of ground on the far side of her woodshed. "How many tents are you setting up?"

"Three, eventually," Nick replied, coming up beside her. "Let's just put the one on the other side of that woodshed for now, Brian. You can get Mike and Dean to do that while you and Spike get the rest of the equipment unloaded. They want to get the big chopper out of here as soon as possible. We'll just leave ours where it is for the time being."

Brian's hazel eyes darted from his boss to Tory, then back again. "She doesn't want the tent over there."

Nick's brow lowered thoughtfully. "How about the base of that rise, then? It shouldn't be visible there." He motioned toward the jagged rocks jutting along the edge of the flatter sweep of land. "Will that be all right with you, Tory?"

There was a familiarity in his tone that seemed to surprise Brian. Tory couldn't help noticing the smile in Nick's eyes when he looked down at her.

"That's fine," she replied, locking her knees so they wouldn't buckle.

"Good. Get the men started on it, will you?" he asked Brian. "I'll be over to help in a minute."

Brian jogged off, unaware that his back was being used as a focal point for deep brown eyes purposely avoiding a pair of disturbing turquoise ones.

"I got most of the supplies you wanted." Nick's glance swept her face and settled on her hands. "But there were a few things we couldn't get—painkillers, antibiotics. The guy Brian talked to at the pharmaceutical house said he'd fill your order as soon as we give him your vendor number."

Tory was watching his hands. He was pulling them out of his gloves. "I'll get it for you. I forgot about their being controlled substances. When you call, would you mind ordering something else for me, too? Anna Dorvak needs anti-inflammatories for her arthritis."

"I'll see what I can do. Here." He held out his gloves. "Put these on. I'll go get another pair."

Tory felt herself take a mental step backward, though all she really did was move her glance to his jaw. He must have shaved at Albert's. "That's okay. Mine are just inside and you'll need—"

His interruption was gentle. "I want to get a thinner pair anyway. Some of that equipment is hard enough to set up without having trouble hanging on to a screwdriver. These are too bulky." Ducking his head slightly so he could see her eyes, which were now riveted on the gloves, he moved closer. "Take them, Tory."

They were only gloves. Totally inanimate objects. Yet there seemed to be something symbolic in his gesture. Just as there would be if she took them.

Slowly she raised her hand, leaving it suspended over his. Then, her fingers folded over the smooth leather.

The warmth of his skin clung to the thick fur lining, folding over her fingers as she slipped them on. "Thank you," she whispered past the odd constriction in her throat. That tightness only increased when she looked back up at him.

"You're welcome." He smiled, then a moment later turned away.

Tory touched an enormously oversized finger to her mouth—and another brick bit the dust.

The activity outside came to a halt with the rapidly approaching dusk. All of the villagers had returned to their homes, but Tory wasn't alone.

Flannel shirts, jeans and heavy boots seemed to be the uniform of the five men filling her small kitchen and living room. Every one of those men looked more like a lumberjack than a scientist. Their easy banter filled the air with deep, masculine laughter, the sound of Nick's throaty chuckle more noticeable for its infrequency.

Dean Wasco, the bulky, slightly cantankerous seismologist who must have come from somewhere in Texas, leaned over Tory's shoulder, watching her flatten hunks of *aladika* dough. "I think I can handle that, ma'am," he drawled, his beefy hand disappearing into the bowl. "Looks sort of like the Indian fry bread we make back home in Lubbock."

Suspicion confirmed. He was from Texas.

Having no choice but to relinquish her task, she turned to find Nick presenting her with a cup of coffee. "Why don't you take a break?" he suggested with that little half smile of his, and indicated the stool next to the one Brian occupied with a nod of his head.

He didn't see how tightly her fingers curled around the cup she'd just accepted. His glance had darted to the man sitting on the floor beside the rickety old chairs.

"This really is great, Dr. Richards." Mike Lindley, the only member of the crew under thirty, shoved his wire-rimmed glasses up on his nose and cut into the chunk of sea lion on his plate. "I thought for sure we'd be eating something out of a can tonight."

"You probably will be after tonight," Brian informed him, reaching across the counter to grab a piece of the hot *aladika*. "I'm supposed to draw up a roster in the morning. We'll all get our turn at K.P."

"Ugh!"

That descriptive comment came from the balding man who'd just plopped his lanky frame down on the sofa, his heaping plate now balanced on his knee. He'd been introduced to Tory as Sherman Towerman, a geophysicist from West Virginia. The men called him "Spike."

"Don't sound so enthusiastic," Brian laughed. "Even our esteemed boss gets a shot at it."

Nick, now leaning against the counter on the other side of Brian, smiled easily. "Better put my name at the end of your K.P. list. That way I'll know what I have to fix to get even with you guys."

"Oh, wonderful." Dean dropped another hunk of dough into the sputtering oil. "That means we'll get rock stew again."

"Rock stew?" Mike, the apparent newcomer to the team, glanced over the rim of his glasses at Nick. He had just voiced Tory's thought perfectly.

"You'll recognize it if he decides to make it." Dean grinned. "The shells'll give it away. Hey, Tory, you're not eatin'. Want me to fix you a plate?"

"No, thanks." Cradling her mug between her hands, she offered him a warm smile. "I'm not hungry." Not hungry enough to eat sea lion, anyway.

Dean tossed a piece of bread onto a plate and pushed it across the counter, apparently understanding her problem. "Eat up, girl. Can't have our doctor gettin' sick now, can we, Nick?"

Nick shook his head gravely, his lips twitching as he watched Tory eye the piece of meat Dean had just added to her plate. Dean hadn't understood her reluctance after all.

"This is great. Really great." Mike enthusiastically bit into the meat. "Where'd you get the beef? They told me it was more precious than gold up here."

"It's not beef." Nick took his eyes off Tory long enough to glance over at Mike. "It's sea lion."

Mike halted mid chew, his fork clattering to his plate. With apparent difficulty, he swallowed. "Sea lion?" he squeaked. "You mean one of those cute little things with the flippers?"

"Yep." Spike was anything but verbose.

Squinting through his glasses, Mike stared thoughtfully at what was left of his meal. After due consideration, he polished off the last bite. Apparently he'd decided that the nature of the beast didn't matter after all.

"You really picked up native cooking in a hurry, Tory." Brian sopped up the last of his gravy with a piece of bread and popped it into his mouth. "If this isn't fixed right, it can taste like fishy rubber."

"Actually—" Tory leveled her eyes at the head that had just ducked behind Brian's "—Nick and Katrina Nuclief are responsible for it. I just helped."

The only response she heard was the solemnly delivered "Touché" that came from the opposite end of the counter.

She turned her smile to her cup.

Maybe it would be all right after all. She and Nick seemed to have got past a barrier of some kind. His attitude toward her ever since this afternoon had been no different from that of the rest of the crew—friendly and quite accepting. Maybe they could just work together and she could forget everything that had happened up until now.

If you believe that, she chided herself when Nick brushed her arm a while later, you're the sucker they were looking for when they tried to sell that swampland in Florida.

He'd barely touched her, the contact seeming quite accidental. But accidental or not, she'd felt it all the way to her toes.

Nick however, hadn't seemed to notice anything extraordinary about it. Tory didn't know if it was relief she felt at that or disappointment.

Two weeks later, she still hadn't figured it out.

Five

The two crew members who hadn't come with the rest of Nick's men had arrived, only to be dispatched to one of the other islands with Dean before Tory could meet them. She hadn't been particularly pleased with that. If she was going to take care of these men, she was going to do it right, and that meant getting some information from them. It wasn't as though she wanted to do complete physicals. All she wanted was enough information to avoid botching any potential treatment. It would hardly help to give penicillin to a man who was allergic or to think stomach pains were a bad appendix if the thing had already been removed. Mike, Brian and Spike had seen the obvious wisdom of her request and willingly complied. Nick saw it, too, and promised to send Dean and the new arrivals to her as soon as they returned. As for himself, he kept avoiding the issue by saying he was too busy.

Right now, Tory had to admit that Nick was indeed busy.

She stood outside the prefabricated metal building the men had erected a short distance from their heavy canvas tent. The men's tent was actually larger than her cabin, and the metal building just missed being the size of an airplane hanger. The men called it "the garage."

How they'd got a jeep and three snowmobiles into the transport helicopter to get them here was anybody's guess. How Tory was supposed to help Nick fix the jeep was also open to considerable speculation.

Directing a grimace at the ooze creeping over the tops of her boots—a mucky combination of mud and slushy snow—she posed her inquiry to the legs sticking out from under the jeep. "Don't you think it'd be easier to fix that if you moved it inside?"

Nick was lying on a tarp under the very utilitarian vehicle. "Probably," came his disembodied and rather droll reply. "But it didn't break down in there. Hand me a nine-sixteenths socket, will you?"

Tory glanced behind her, hoping to see one of the men emerge from a building. She knew that most of them were gone and whoever was here wasn't anywhere in sight.

She frowned at the toolbox beside the front tire. "What does it look like?" Screwdrivers, pliers and wrenches she could identify. A nine-sixteenths socket was beyond her expertise.

"Like this." A greasy tool poked out from just below the door. "It's the top part. Only I need a bigger one."

"I suppose if I'd grown up a boy I'd have learned all this stuff by osmosis." Nothing resembling what she was looking for was in the top of the box, and she started digging around in the bottom. "Are you sure it's in here?"

Nick's very patient "Yes" sounded as though it had a grin tacked on it. "And I'm glad you didn't grow up as a boy."

Smiling at his teasing, she finally produced the proper part. "Here it is," she announced, and slapped it with surgical precision into the palm of his outstretched hand.

"Ouch! You're supposed to be assisting me, not trying to break my fingers."

She hadn't hit him that hard. "Sorry," she mumbled, not sounding particularly apologetic. "Occupational hazard."

"Apology, such as it was, accepted. Now, scoot under here. I need you to hold this for me."

Having no idea what "this" was, and not too enamored of the idea of crawling under the jeep, she peered at its mud-caked underside. Nick's face was little more than a shadow, most of the light coming from the flashlight lying next to him. That was apparently what he wanted her to hold.

"Do I have to?" She wasn't very crazy about the idea of lying down on that tarp next to Nick, either. Though he hadn't made a single attempt to touch her since the day his men had arrived, she didn't want to risk rocking her emotional boat. "I mean, can't I just hold it from here?"

"Not unless you've just grown three-foot arms. Come on. You won't get muddy. The tarp's dry."

So was her throat. And it wasn't just from the cold air she was breathing.

You can handle this, she coached herself, and tried to figure out how she was supposed to accomplish this little feat. There didn't appear to be any graceful way to get under the jeep, so there wasn't much sense pretending otherwise.

Flattening herself out, she wriggled across the tarp. "This isn't exactly in my job description."

"I just extended your responsibilities to sick jeeps." Moving over to give himself arm room, he handed her the flashlight. "Point it up here."

She did as he'd instructed, noting the concentration furrowing his brow when he twisted his ratchet around something she couldn't identify. There was a streak of grease running from the side of his nose across his cheek. Tory had to force herself not to pick up the rag lying by his head and wipe it away. She didn't dare touch him.

He'd barely looked at her, but the sensual tension that could spark between them with little more than a glance was something almost tangible. It was there now, constricting every muscle in her body and tightening the firm line of his mouth. Nick hadn't done a thing to capitalize on that tension—not overtly, anyway. Simply by withholding physical contact, he was making her ache for something she kept telling herself she didn't want. Tory had the feeling he knew exactly how effective his strategy was.

That tactic, however, didn't appear to be without its drawbacks. Nick's voice sounded awfully husky when he asked her to hold the light a little steadier.

"You two really should stop meeting like this." Brian's boots materialized only seconds before his curly brown head appeared at the edge of the chassis. "What's going on under here?"

Oh, I'm just thinking about having a stroke, Tory joked to herself as she heard Nick grumble, "Nothing exciting. Just trying to fix this damn transmission."

Brian scowled. "I'll take care of it. You've got a bigger problem. Dean radioed in from a few miles away. He's coming back with Les and that Dr. Fancy Pants."

"It's Clancy Shants," Nick corrected, frowning at the condescension in Brian's tone. "Why're they coming back now? They're supposed to be out for the rest of the week."

Nick had already pushed himself to the side of the tarp. She saw Brian's hand come down to pull Nick to his feet. Seconds later, Brian offered her the same assistance.

Though she was standing between the two men, she wasn't really paying much attention to what Brian was saying—something about an argument between this Dr. Shants and the other guy. She was staring down at the grease the flashlight had left on her hands.

"You can wash up in there," Nick advised her, interrupting Brian to motion toward the men's sleeping quarters. "There's some turpentine in the bathroom just inside the door."

Brian was talking again, leaving her with nothing to do but head for the men's tent. She didn't want to stick around anyway. It was so much easier to pretend Nick didn't affect her when there was a little distance between them. Fifty feet wasn't enough. As she reached the door of the tent, she could still feel Nick's eyes sending those icy-hot tingles down her back. It was getting to be a familiar sensation.

Out of sight was hardly out of mind, but she breathed a sigh of relief when she stepped inside and closed the heavy canvas flap behind her. She'd never been in the men's tent before, but she paused only long enough to search out the bathroom. It was the small, curtained-off area to her left. Washing up quickly, she stepped back out into the room.

Cots were lined neatly on either side, and a not-so-neat assortment of books, shaving kits and potato-chip bags occupied the crates that served as night-stands. A heavy green sweater was tossed across the foot of the cot at the far end. Peeking out from under it was the sleeve of the plaid shirt Nick had been wearing the day his plane had brought him crashing into her life.

A tiny smile tugged the corners of her mouth. That cot had to be Nick's, but it looked so narrow for his long, broad-shouldered frame. The double bed she slept in would be so much better suited for...

Giving her head a sharp shake, she started to turn. The sight of the brightly colored quilt folded on the crate by that cot stopped her.

That quilt belonged to Willy, and it was a poignant reminder of what had happened only three days ago. It was such a little thing really—except to that young boy. And Tory used to be so good at blocking even the little things out. Now she remembered it as if it had just happened.

She'd been in her cabin, trying to master the first chord on her balalaika, when the sound of the jeep roaring around the hill announced Nick's return. He'd been gone for two days. The unwanted thrill of anticipation shooting through her had been immediately diagnosed as nothing more than heartburn—which had threatened to turn to heart failure when she heard the tentative knock on her door a few minutes later,

Anticipation had died the instant she'd opened the door. It wasn't Nick. It was Willy. He had Kai, his tiny puppy, wrapped in his best quilt and was hugging him to his chest. The anguish in the boy's glistening black eyes had sliced through her with frightening swiftness. One look at his grief-stricken face had told her she didn't have to ask what was wrong.

"I'm so sorry, Willy," she'd whispered, gently removing the lifeless bundle from his arms. "But it's better now. He doesn't have to fight anymore." The puppy had never been strong, though Willy had wanted desperately to believe otherwise.

The stoicism revealed in Willy's tightly pressed lips had been almost harder for Tory to handle than his tears would have been.

Placing the bundle on the step beside her as she sat down, she'd watched Willy touch the corner of the blanket. Tory's heart had twisted. Why hadn't she been able to repress the empathy she'd been feeling? Willy had needed her to be strong, yet she'd felt anything but that.

Willy's hand had jerked back and he'd blinked hard. "I didn't want him anyway."

Her smile hadn't been the professional one she had hidden behind so often before. It had been tremulous, unguarded. And her softly spoken words had been filled with compassion. "You don't mean that, Willy. It just hurts so much right now that you—"

"No!" he'd sobbed, jumping back when she touched his shoulder. "I...I hate him!" He'd whirled around and ran, frantically trying to escape the feelings he couldn't quite understand.

She had seen Nick round the cabin just moments before. He'd stopped, watching. But it hadn't been his quiet "Let him go" when she started after the child that had brought her to a halt. It had been the sight of Albert, who had just appeared at the base of the hill and was racing after his son.

The ever-present breeze had been throwing thick strands of her hair across her face. Pushing them back, her eyes on the father and son now huddled together, she'd felt Nick come up behind her. "He said he hated Kai," she'd observed, more to herself than to Nick. "But I know he loved that puppy."

"I heard," had come the reply from a scant foot away. "They were just words, though. We all use them to convince ourself that something doesn't matter. He knows how he really felt about him."

In the back of her mind, a question had formed. What words had Nick used to convince himself that something didn't matter?

The inquiry had been banished as quickly as it had arisen. "But he's too young to be denying his feelings like that."

"Meaning it's only when you're old enough to understand what you're denying that it's all right?"

Hearing a trace of accusation in his question, she'd turned around—and immediately wished she hadn't. The jolt of meeting the eyes that had haunted her dreams, coming so quickly on the heels of the ache she felt for Willy, had threatened to shatter her already questionable calm.

Withdrawing from his searching glance, she'd started to scramble behind the part of her wall that allowed her to hide from the oddly escalating ache. But those particular bricks had all fallen down.

She'd tried to pretend otherwise. "As a doctor, I know it's never healthy to reject your emotions."

His right hand—the one she'd chosen to look at so she wouldn't have to look at him—had disappeared into the pocket of his heavy jacket. "Then, doctor," he'd urged quietly, holding out a small box containing the drugs she'd requested for Anna Dorvak, "heal thyself."

In stunned silence, she'd clutched the small parcel and watched Nick carefully pick up the bundle on her step.

There was another old adage she could have used to counter him with. Didn't he know that the physician who treated herself had a fool for a patient?

The distinctive whir of a helicopter sliced through her thoughts. Glancing down at the quilt she held against her chest, she erased the pensive frown from her forehead and hurried outside. Since Dean and the other men had just arrived, she'd tell Nick later that she'd give the quilt back to Willy's mother.

Nick and Brian were at the chopper and Tory was picking her way between patches of snow and mud puddles when she heard Nick yelling at her. Well, he wasn't exactly yelling at her. It was just that shouting was the only way he could be heard over the roar of the rotors.

"What?" she called back. She couldn't hear a thing he was saying, though he was only thirty yards away.

He cupped his hands around his mouth. "I'm sending these guys up to see you."

"What's wrong?" It felt as though she was screaming.

Nick didn't answer immediately. The scowl creasing his grimly set features intensified when the two men she'd yet to meet stepped off the chopper and Brian hustled them toward the tent she'd just left. "Nothing major," he finally hurled back. "Looks like a bashed face and some bruised knuckles. Don't know what else. Ten minutes. Okay?"

"Okay," she mumbled to herself, and quickened her pace. What on earth had happened out there? Brian said the men had had an argument, but it sounded more like a fistfight.

Which was exactly what it turned out to be.

The two men Dean brought to her cabin were quite subdued—until she started working on them. The guy named Les was huge, and the biggest baby she'd ever met. The entire time she'd been bandaging his knuckles he'd done nothing but whine. Some six-year-olds were more cooperative.

Clancy Shants, she decided after he'd warned her for the third time that the tiny scrape on his forehead better not leave a scar, was an obstreperous little twerp. He was more concerned about his face—which she might have thought attractive if he hadn't so obviously thought so himself—than the sprained wrist she'd taped.

The bashed face belonged to Dean. He'd intercepted a couple of punches Les had meant for Clancy. Trying to break up the fight had earned the easygoing Texan a few more features.

She had just sent Dean on his way with a patch over what was going to be a very colorful right eye when her cabin door creaked open. Nick, looking considerably calmer than she'd last seen him, poked his head inside. "How'd it go?"

With the door open she could hear the drone of the helicopter disappearing in the distance. Dean had mentioned that Nick had fired the two men. Brian was taking them back to the mainland.

"No problem," she returned, gathering up the supplies she hadn't used to put them back in the storage room. "What happened, anyway?" And why is it, she asked herself when he stepped inside, that whenever he's in here, this cabin seems so much smaller?

The glow of the lamps seemed even more intimate now, though there was still a fair amount of gray daylight coming through the windows. Something about him made her notice the most insignificant things.

"I'm sure you don't want a blow-by-blow account," he said, straight-faced, and joined her at the counter. Picking up odds and ends of bandage wrappers, he tossed them into the stove as he continued, "Basically, it's a case of two men who each think they're more important than the other. I had reservations about both of them. So did Craig. But their credentials were excellent and . . ." The shrug completing his sentence was anything but dismissing. He blamed himself for having made a judgment error, and if Tory was reading him right, he was also feeling guilty about what had happened to Dean. "These things just happen sometimes."

She couldn't help wondering who he was trying to convince. "Obviously. But you'd think they could have worked out their differences some other way."

"Apparently those two couldn't." Handing her a roll of gauze, he accepted the pieces of wadded-up tape she held out to him. "A lot of it has to do with this place, I suppose. The remoteness or the rawness.

Whatever it is, it strips a person, reduces you to your most basic feelings.''

"That's absurd," she muttered. "They're men, not animals."

"I said feelings, Tory. Not instincts. I'm not saying we revert to apes; it's more like you can't hide from yourself here."

The clank of the stove's door being closed after he'd tossed in the last of the scraps seemed to punctuate his conviction.

"Those guys are both professors," he continued evenly. "Neither one had ever been exposed to anything like this before. They were used to the protection of academia and a life that proscribed a certain kind of behavior. Some people can't handle the changes this kind of expedition forces on you." He shook his head. "I've never seen anything like this happen after such a short time, though. Are these Brian's?"

A pair of aviator-type sunglasses were suspended between his fingers.

If Nick hadn't changed the subject, she would have. Though he'd been using the impersonal "you" while he'd been talking, his words were hitting a little too close to home.

Already halfway down the hall, and wondering if now wouldn't be a good time to get the medical information she needed from him, she confirmed that the glasses did belong to Brian. He'd left them on the counter when he'd come to get the two men. "I don't know why he had them," she called back, putting the things she'd carried into the storage room back on the shelf. "We haven't had any sun for days."

Nick apparently didn't mind carrying on a conversation with someone he couldn't see. "He needs them when he's flying," he explained, reminding her that Brian was now doing just that. "If the sun does come out while you're up there, it gets pretty bright. There's an extra pair of mine in the chopper, though. He can use 'em if he needs 'em."

Encouraged by Nick's casual tone, she took a deep breath and headed back into the hall. Without quite knowing why, she knew her request was going to meet with resistance.

"As long as you're here—" she laid a pad of preprinted forms down on the counter in front of him "—you can fill this out. And don't tell me you're busy right now."

Nick frowned down at the forms. They were the kind a person usually fills out the first time he sees a doctor. The only reason Tory had them was that they'd been packed with her books and not the supplies that had wound up in storage.

He carried his frown to her face. "I've got to fix the jeep."

"Brian said he'd take care of it."

"He's busy."

That was true. "Can't the jeep wait? This'll only take a few minutes."

"Is this really necessary?" he grumbled, crossing his arms over the black stripe woven across his pale blue ski sweater.

When his question met her confirming nod, he seemed to reconsider his inexplicably stubborn position. Reconsider but not relent. The devilish gleam slipping into his eyes told her he wasn't ready to give in just yet. "You know I'm healthy, doctor. And since nothing's going to happen to me, I don't think it's necessary to subject me to your examination."

The breath she drew this time was one of exasperation—or maybe courage. It was taking a considerable amount of that not to shy from the gaze wandering from where her hand curved at the base of her throat to where her breast pressed against her forearm.

"You're not invincible," she pointed out. The way he was now looking at her mouth made her terribly conscious of his. It was parted slightly, as if he'd just sucked in a deep breath of his own. "I'm only trying to do the job you asked me to do. None of your men made a fuss about answering a few questions and having their blood pressure taken."

"I'm not making a fuss about anything. I just don't think it's...oh, hell," he sighed, reaching for the pad. "Give me a pen."

Handing him the one she was holding, she stepped away when he turned and slid onto the stool. It wasn't the sight of his head bent intently over the form that made her forget about the item she'd meant to retrieve from the storage room. It was the distracting width of his shoulders and the long line of his back. It had been only a little over two weeks since she'd felt the strength in the muscles hidden beneath his sweater. Two weeks that seemed like a lifetime.

That odd knot was forming in her stomach again. All she'd have to do was reach out and...

"Done," he pronounced moments later, quite effectively derailing her train of thought, and tossed the pen aside.

A bit of her usual efficiency was missing when she quickly scanned the form. She barely noted that he'd had all the usual childhood diseases, had no history of familial illness and was thirty-seven years old.

Dropping the pad back on the counter, she cleared her throat. "I'll get your blood pressure now."

Nick's decisive "No," when she started toward the storage room to get the sphygmomanometer and cuff she'd forgotten brought her to a halt.

Puzzled by the terseness of that response and his enigmatic expression, she asked, "Why not?"

The muscle in his jaw jumped. "That's the part of this 'exam' that isn't necessary. My blood pressure wouldn't be normal right now anyway."

Tory didn't like having to repeat the same question, but she did. "Why not?"

"Because you're not ready."

He must have realized she didn't understand that mysterious little remark, but he didn't look as though he was going to explain it. There were times when he thoroughly baffled her. "I'm not ready for what?"

Drawing his hand through his hair as he stood, he muttered, "What will happen if you so much as touch me."

Tory's heart came to a wild, thudding stop, only to pick up those missed beats with a vengeance when he positioned himself in front of her.

"I've tried my damnedest not to rush you, Tory, but it's getting harder all the time to keep my hands off you. I keep thinking that sooner or later you'll admit there's something between us, but you won't." His hands clenched, mimicking the way the muscle in his jaw jerked again. His eyes beseeched even as they accused. "Why do you keep denying it?"

The question was little more than a whisper. He might as well have screamed it.

Moving backward had flattened her against the wall of cabinets. "Nick, I . . ." Dear God, what should she say? There *was* something between them, and it was more than just a simple physical attraction. It was a crazy kind of telepathy that made verbal communication an unnecessary effort at times because they were already attuned to each other somehow. "There isn't any point in it," she concluded weakly.

It was Nick's turn at incomprehension. "No *point* in it? What the hell's that supposed to mean?"

She was staring at the vein throbbing in his neck. He was right. She probably wouldn't get a very accurate reading of his blood pressure right now. "Just what I said. I'm only going to be here for a year and you'll—"

"You'll have to come up with a better excuse than that," he interrupted, moving closer. The drawer handles bit into her back. "Don't deny us what we both want just because it can't last forever, Tory. We've got a year. Let's just see where it takes us."

It wasn't an excuse. It was a reason. And she knew she should be trying to make him see that. But the intensity in his expression and the feel of his hands cupping her face were making rationality more than a little difficult. "I can't," she breathed, frantically searching for the arguments she couldn't seem to voice.

"How do you know?" His question was spoken against her lips. "You haven't even tried."

A thousand fragmented jolts shot through her. His mouth was barely touching hers, drifting slowly from one corner to the other and taking mind-distorting little sips. I haven't tried, she asked silently, feeling herself opening beneath his gentle touch even as she tried to withdraw from it. I haven't tried to tell myself you don't matter to me? That I don't want you so much it hurts?

Only his hands on her face and the feather-light feel of his mouth held her. She could have moved away. She should. But something inside wouldn't let her. He had said that this place stripped a person, reduced you to your most basic feelings. But it wasn't just this place. It was Nick.

Though she'd done nothing but deny it for days, she'd ached for him. He was proving that to her now, just as he was proving how right he was about what would happen if they touched each other.

His fingers had trailed down her throat to curl over the soft wool covering her arms. Pulling her to his chest, he claimed her in a deep, probing kiss. His hunger was answered with her own, a hunger long suppressed and begging for release.

The warmth of his tongue demanded, withdrew and demanded again. That intrusion was welcomed and returned. She savored the taste of him, the feel of his hands easing from her arms to fold across her back. She knew it was physically impossible for her body to melt, but that's exactly what it seemed to be doing.

Aligning her more intimately to his hard frame, he pressed his fingers to the base of her spine, then seared a heated path up her side to splay them beneath her breast. Gently he lifted its weight, covering her peaked nipple with his palm.

A kittenish whimper snagged in her throat, his lips seeking to still the one that followed when his palm began to move in tantalizing circles. The sensations he elicited only increased with the subtle thrust of his hips. She arched toward him.

This time the groan filtering past the pulse pounding in her ears was his, and a bolt of pure flame shot through her, igniting a fire deep inside.

Beneath her own hands she could feel the muscles in his back growing rigid, the tension in his body a mirror of what he was creating in her. Somehow she had worked her hands beneath his sweater and she felt a spasm shudder his length when her fingers drifted over his smooth flesh.

There was a frantic little voice screaming in the back of her mind, a thread of reason warning her how dangerous her actions were. Each touch of her own encouraged Nick more, increasing the liberties she allowed him to take. The warnings grew fainter.

The husky voice of reason rasping in her ear wasn't the one she had just silenced. It was Nick's. "My God, Tory," he groaned, his breath heavy. "Do you have any idea how hard it's going to be to leave you?"

"To leave me?" she repeated, sounding every bit as dazed as she felt.

His smile was as gentle as the feel of his hands cradling her face. "Don't worry. You're not going to get rid of me for very long. I'll only be out in the field for a couple of weeks, but when I get back—" his thumb caressed her bottom lip, kiss swollen and trembling "—I want an answer."

The breath she inhaled was tremulous and filled her lungs with the scent of fresh air clinging to his sweater, the spiciness of his soap. Everything about him seemed destined to affect her. "What's the question?" she returned in a voice so faint it didn't even sound like her own.

"The one I can see in your eyes, honey. Do you take what you want—what we both want—or keep trying to deny what you feel?'' The pressure of his thumb increased, stilling the response that hadn't had a chance to form. ''I don't want you to answer me now. I want you think about it.''

With that he dropped a debilitatingly tender kiss on her lips and started toward the door. ''And while you're thinking about it,'' he admonished, desire still smoldering in his eyes, ''be honest with yourself.''

Tory blinked at the space where he had stood only a moment ago, the click of the door closing barely audible over the beat of her heart. Whether Nick's powers of perception were even stronger than she'd suspected or he'd just got lucky didn't much matter. He'd just ripped a gaping hole in her best defense—the tactic she'd always used to avoid facing something she didn't want to cope with.

As long as she left a situation ambiguous, a feeling unnamed, she didn't have to deal with it. Now he'd pinned their situation down in terms so concrete she couldn't possibly hide from it anymore. Nick wasn't going to let her.

He wanted her. She wanted him. There was no point pretending otherwise. The question she had to answer was, What was she going to do about it?

Six

Unfortunately, taking a cargo plane to Anchorage and hightailing it back to California was not a viable alternative. She had a responsibility to the villagers she had no intention of walking out on, and she'd never been in the habit of running. Hiding was more her style.

Like an ostrich, she'd stick her head in the sand. The picture that presented to the rest of the world was far from appealing. There was no hole to bury her head in anyway, and what few bricks were left in her wall stood on a very shaky foundation. Nick had said to be honest with herself. That was something she'd learned to avoid. But the ability to delude herself simply wasn't there anymore. It was time to face a few pertinent facts.

Nick had certainly been honest enough with her. They'd known each other for only twelve hours before he'd informed her of his views on permanent re-lationships. "Never could see committing myself to something that won't last anyway," he'd said, rein-forcing that conviction with the words he'd spoken just before he'd left. "Don't deny us what we want just because it can't last forever."

He wanted an affair. Absolutely nothing more.

It had been eleven days since he'd left with the rest of his crew, another three before he was due to re-turn. By now, her little speech had been rehearsed to perfection. Actually, there were two. Which one she was going to use was still up for grabs.

Sitting on the braided rug in front of the sofa, Tory tucked her feet beneath her in a reasonably accurate lotus position and curved her hands, palms up, on her knees. Taking a deep breath, she closed her eyes. It wouldn't hurt to run through those speeches once more.

I'm sorry, Nick. I can't have an affair with you be-cause I've never had an affair in my life and that's the last thing I had in mind when I came here. You've got your work and I've got mine, so let's just be friends and leave it at that.

Exhaling slowly, as the book said to do, she tried the other one.

I'm sorry, Nick. I can't have an affair with you be-cause I think I'm falling in love with you, and if we make love it'll only make it hurt because I know it'll all be over in eleven months, and if you really cared about me you wouldn't be putting a time limit on it just because that's when I'm supposed to leave, and I can't stay when Anton gets back because there wouldn't be any reason for me to, and . . .

Well, so the second speech wasn't quite perfect. It wasn't the one she was going to use anyway—even if it was more honest than the first.

The muscle in her right foot was cramping. Massaging her arch, she decided she'd had enough yoga for one day. The inner peace and tranquillity the book promised could hardly be attained when her body protested the prescribed positions and her mind was occupied with thoughts that were anything but calming.

The realization, and the admission, that she was falling in love with Nick hadn't come abruptly. It was more a case of already knowing but not wanting to know. To Tory that had made perfect sense. She couldn't identify any particular time or incident that had made it happen, but when Nick left, it felt as though he'd taken a part of her with him.

Don't get maudlin, she warned herself, and with a groan lifted herself up from the floor. Her foot wasn't the only thing with a cramp in it. The muscles protesting now were the ones she'd used tilling her garden.

Kneeling on the sofa, elbows propped on the sill and chin cupped in her hand, she stared out the window and wondered how long it would take her radishes to sprout.

The weather had been clear most of the week. As clear as it ever got in the Aleutians, anyway. And the temperature had finally crept up into the low forties. There wasn't much snow left, just a stray patch or two. The thick tufts of windswept grass were dew-heavy with the fog that had enveloped the island a few hours ago, but she knew the cold frame she'd built would protect her seeds. At least, her book on solar gardening said it would. She could use another sheet of heavy plastic, though. Maybe Nick would—

Giving her head a sharp shake—wasn't there anything she could think about that didn't somehow include him—she started to pull away from the window. Instead, she leaned forward and squinted through the rain-stained glass.

The fog gave a ghostlike appearance to the two male shapes approaching her cabin from the direction of the camp. They seemed to be leaning against each other.

Tory's brow furrowed. There was no way she would have missed the noise of the helicopter. Whether or not she heard the jeep usually depended on which way the wind was blowing. Nick had left in the jeep.

Her heart, which had been pumping in nice, regular beats, took an erratic lurch and doubled its tempo. Tugging her oversize white sweater over the hips of her snug burgundy cords, her sock-covered feet hit the floor. Arms crossed against the damp chill seeping inside, she planted herself in the doorway and watched Brian and Nick emerge through the soupy mist.

Nick's arm was draped over Brian's shoulder. Brian was cradling his left arm with his right.

Stifling the urge to rush out and throw her arms around Nick—which would hardly lend any credence to the speech she had to deliver—she pushed her inquiry past the pulse in her throat. "What happened?"

Brian disengaged himself from Nick's support. "I fell into some rocks. Nick seems to think you should take a look at my arm."

"You're going to have to do more than look at it." Concern shadowed Nick's expression, but there was a welcoming smile in his eyes when he glanced at Tory.

Trying not to think about her inconsistent heartbeat or the crazy flip-flop her stomach had done the instant she'd heard Nick's voice, she stepped back for the men to enter. "Why don't you sit over there?" She motioned Brian to the nearest stool, deliberately keeping her back to Nick.

He'd looked different somehow. More rugged, untamed. Maybe it was the week's worth of heavy brown beard shaping the chiseled line of his jaw. Or maybe she was just seeing him differently because she'd realized...

Now was not the time to think about it. Brian needed her. "Let's get you out of that jacket."

With her help, Brian shrugged out of his torn parka. He couldn't roll up his shirt sleeve, though. It was ripped and soaked with blood from the wound on his forearm, and the flannel was stuck to some of the injured tissue.

"I'm going to have to cut this off," she mumbled, gingerly lifting some of the material away.

Brian's eyes went wide. "My arm?"

"No, Brian. Your shirt. Your arm will be just fine. I'll be right back." Smiling at his relief, she headed into the storage room.

When she returned with the things she thought she'd need, Brian was frowning at the long flannel sleeve that was about to become a short one. Nick was sitting on the arm of the sofa, his head turned away as he stared out the window.

Wanting to keep her mind on her task and Brian's off it, she asked him what he'd been doing when he injured himself and began carefully to clean the wound.

"We were boring holes in the permafrost to set some instruments—" A tiny hiss was sucked between his teeth. She'd just injected an anesthetic. The gash was going to require a few stitches. "I backed over the side of a cliff. Well, not exactly a cliff, but it sure seemed like it at the time..."

Tory tried to listen while Brian rattled on, but she was more concerned about the way his arm jerked each time she inserted the small, curved needle. His hand was shaking, too. Probably from nerves. "I know you're doing the best you can," she consoled him when his arm jumped again. "But this'll go a lot faster if we could hold you still. Why don't you try looking the other way?"

She'd given him enough anesthetic to numb him from his wrist to his elbow, so she knew his reaction was only psychological and not from any additional pain she was inflicting. She'd seen the phenomenon often enough to appreciate it. Brian's efforts were appreciated, too. He was trying to do as she suggested, but he couldn't seem to keep his eyes off his arm.

Tory looked over at Nick, who seemed fascinated with the cracks in the wall beside him. "Would you help me for a minute?" Then to Brian, she added, "He owes me for the assist I gave him with the jeep."

Brian offered her a sheepishly apologetic smile. "I tried."

With obvious reluctance Nick abandoned his survey of the architectural defects of her cabin. "What do you want me to do?"

"Hold his arm."

Nick did as she asked, keeping his head averted. She wished Brian would do the same. Every time he jerked his arm, Nick jerked, too. And though Brian's stoic features were a little on the pale side, Nick looked worse.

"There," she pronounced finally. "All finished."

She'd meant the encouragement for Brian, but it was Nick who let out the tight little sigh.

"You can let go now, Nick. You're cutting off his circulation."

Brian wiggled his fingers and stared at the veins bulging on the back of his hand. "It does look a little blue, doesn't it?"

Without saying a word to the two people staring questioningly at him, Nick released his death grip and walked back to the sofa. Keeping his back to them, he reclaimed his perch on its arm.

"Thanks, doc," Brian said after she'd taped a thick pad of gauze over her handiwork. "I know it's only noon, but I think I'll go lie down for a while."

"That's probably a good idea, but have Nick walk back with you."

He shook his wiry brown curls. "I don't think he'd better go anywhere. He doesn't look too good."

A moment later, accompanied by her reminder to keep his bandage dry, Brian let himself out.

Tory leaned across the counter, trying to see more of Nick's face than just his profile. Brian was right. Nick didn't look very good. "Are you all right?"

The last time she'd asked him that, he'd mumbled, "Of course I am," and promptly passed out.

"I'm fine." The deep breath he took seemed to indicate otherwise, and the question he directed to the wall sounded a bit weak. "How do you do it?"

There was no reason to ask what he was talking about. "I try not to think about it." Watching him through her lowered lashes while she cleared off the counter, she wondered if it was just the light coming through the curtains that tinted Nick's skin or if he really was a rather pale shade of green. "Are you sure you're okay? I've got some brandy if you want it. Or fresh air might—"

"I said I'm fine." Shoving his fingers through the windblown and fog-damp hair tumbling over his forehead, he took another chest-expanding breath and pushed himself to his feet. He didn't look as though he was going to fall over, and the color in his cheeks looked a lot healthier when he moved away from those curtains. "Did I see a pan of cinnamon rolls by the sink?"

"Uh-huh. I made them this morning. You must be feeling better if you can think about food."

"What makes you think there's anything wrong?"

"Oh, come on, Nick." She tossed a handful of gauze wrappers into the stove and turned to find him leaning quite nonchalantly against the counter. "Don't you think I recognize a case of the squeams when I see it?"

"Squeams?"

"Sure. You know—squeamish. It's nothing to be embarrassed about. Happens to the best of us."

"I didn't think it ever happened to doctors."

"Of course it does," she chuckled, rinsing her hands and pulling open a cabinet to get a plate. "We just don't go around advertising it, that's all. You want a cup of coffee?"

Heart rate at a comfortable sixty beats per minute and the butterflies in her stomach on temporary hold, Tory filled two cups after Nick nodded in the affirmative. He didn't seem in any hurry to bring up their last conversation, and he was steering the discussion now along a safe enough path.

"I noticed the cold frame outside. Did you build it by yourself?"

"All by myself," she repeated, sliding a plate of gooey rolls in front of him. The pride she felt at having completed that project was evident in her eyes, if not her voice. "All the seeds are in, too."

His eyes flickered with amusement as he glanced at her over the cinnamon roll that was about to become history. "Think they'll grow?"

"If they know what's good for them, they will. If they don't, I can always dig 'em up and roast 'em."

Half the roll was gone, washed down with a gulp of coffee. His color was looking better by the minute. *He* was looking better by the minute.

Tory's glance darted from his eyes to her mug just as he repeated, "Roast them?"

"Well, the squash seeds, anyway."

"Your ingenuity never ceases to amaze me, doctor. Which reminds me, how's the lady with the arthritis doing?"

Tory had mentioned Anna only once, and the fact that Nick asked about the elderly lady was ... nice. "Better, thanks to the drugs. There's nothing particularly ingenious about that on my part, though. It's a known treatment."

"The ingenuity I was referring to had more to do with things like that splint you built for Craig's leg and the ramp you rigged up out of that old door to shove the propane tanks around. Want a bite?"

She was about to say no when she saw the other roll she'd put on his plate suspended an inch from her mouth. Why not, she said to herself with a mental shrug, sinking her teeth into the raisin-filled pastry. Now that the butterflies weren't battering her insides, she did feel a little hungry. The other thing she felt was slightly puzzled.

"You know," Nick continued, tearing another hunk off the roll to pop into his mouth, "these aren't half-bad. You make them from scratch?"

She was leaning against the kitchen-side of the counter. Nick occupied the stool on the living-room side, facing her. When he'd come into the cabin with Brian a while ago, she'd thought he looked a little different. But that wasn't really it at all. He actually *seemed* different, yet still the same.

That's not exactly one of your more precise observations, she told herself as she swallowed, then sent a look of tempered indulgence sailing across the pink surface. "You know better than that. They're from a mix, compliments of the Pillsbury Doughboy. Are the rest of the guys still on the other side of the island? I didn't hear the helicopter."

He shook his head and polished off the last of the roll with obvious appreciation for the talents of the puffy little fellow in white. "Mike, Dean and Spike took the chopper over to Umnak. We want to try to tap down on Okmok Caldera, but it'll be a few more days before we get all the readings. There's a lot of potential under there. I missed you."

The question she was about to ask about what he just mentioned died on her lips.

Nick continued as if he hadn't just sent the unsuspecting butterflies winging their way through her midsection. Funny how just hearing him say he missed her could do something like that.

"Brian and I will probably be gone before they get back. We've got to finish the survey to see how much the land mass shifted with the tremors they had here last winter. So far, it doesn't look like there was much movement." His laconic gaze settled on her mouth, and she saw his lips curve in that disarming little half smile of his. "Might as well use the time while Brian's resting up to unscramble my notes so it won't be so hard to write the report later. Come here. You've got icing on your face."

Nick's habit of bouncing from one subject to another, she'd decided, probably had something to do with the complexities of the man himself. His mind was always working—sorting, seeking, discarding and storing. It was hard enough trying to keep up with his conversational shifts without having the distraction of the gentle laughter in his eyes.

Her hand had lifted to brush away the crumb he was looking at, but it never reached her face. He caught it in midair.

"I'll get it." His smile deepened, and he gave her wrist a tug.

Tory's vision blurred as his head inched closer, meeting her halfway across the counter. Before she had a chance to realize what he was going to do, his tongue had captured the errant bit of frosting clinging to the corner of her mouth.

She froze.

Nick leaned closer. "I better make sure there isn't any on the other side." His breath feathered over her face, filling her lungs with his scent when he trailed his tongue over her bottom lip to gently probe the other corner. "Better check up here, too." The silky-rough texture of his tongue followed the velvety outline of her upper lip, then dipped to taste the warm membrane behind it on the return journey.

He still held her hand between them, and her fingers curled, mimicking her toes. "Nick, I—"

"Shhh." Mumbling against her lips, he added, "I'm busy."

Her free hand gripped the counter.

The nibbling kisses he was brushing back and forth over her breathlessly parted mouth were carried along her cheek, touching the lowered lashes of her eyes, the soft skin at her temples. She felt his fingers trace her jaw before they pushed back the heavy ebony hair covering her ear and his tongue circled the shape of her lobe.

The butterflies went completely haywire.

"You're too far away," he breathed.

Tory swallowed. "I think I'd better stay here."

"I'll come over there, then."

"No."

"Why not?"

"Because."

His throaty chuckle vibrated against her ear. "'Because' is a lousy reason. You'll have to do better than that."

She knew she would, but at the moment she couldn't seem to come up with the rationale that would make him stop. All she could think about was the crazy things he was doing to her ear.

"Well?" he prodded, nipping lightly at the curve of her jaw when her head tipped back.

Well what? It took a considerable effort to bring her head forward again. "Uh...we're supposed to be talking."

"That's not a reason." The skin on her neck still tingled even though he'd drawn back. He kissed the tips of her fingers and laid her hand down on the counter. "But if you want to talk, go ahead."

Better. It was definitely better when he wasn't touching her. She could think now. It was time to deliver her little speech.

Or so she thought, until hc skirted the counter and came up behind her. He clasped his hands around her waist. "What do you want to talk about?" This time the scratchy softness of his beard tickled the back of her neck.

Trying to ignore the way his lips were brushing along her nape, she pressed her stomach against the counter. Nick moved with her. "A couple of things. I have this idea I want to tell you about, and you and I need to... Will you please stop it? We can't talk when you're doing that!"

"Sure we can," he refuted, nuzzling her ear again. "At least, we can if you'll stop squirming. You were saying?"

Think, Tory, her normally logical mind screamed. And not about the part of his anatomy you were just squirming against, either! She stood perfectly still. "I was saying that we...ohh!"

"You're not concentrating," he admonished, smiling against her neck.

How was she supposed to concentrate when his hand pressed under her breasts like that? "And you're not listening to me!"

"Sure I am. So far you've said that we have to talk. That you and I...something or other. You didn't finish that part. And you have an idea about something. All rather vague, really. You're usually more articulate than that. But, honest, I heard every word. Now, what do you want to tell me?''

The mind-distorting kisses that were creeping over the side of her throat were making rational thought next to impossible. So was the feel of his hands turning her around and slipping up her back. She wouldn't let herself think about what the pressure of his arousal was doing to her, let alone the lingering kiss he was subjecting her to.

How could she tell him anything when his mouth was moving against hers like this? How could she make him see how impossible a relationship between them was when all she could see was a million shooting stars dancing over the back of her eyelids? Everything seemed so out of kilter, as though she was standing on the edge of the earth and those stars were beckoning her over the edge.

She felt his back go rigid, either from the feel of her hands or from the natural tension caused by his slight backward movement.

"Tell you what," he said, his voice considerably huskier when he pulled from the kiss that had left them both clinging to each other for support. "I'm going to check on Brian and, uh, take a shower. That'll give you some time to remember whatever it was you wanted to tell me."

Tory nodded and drew a shaky hand through her hair. "Since it's just you and Brian, would you like to come back here for dinner?"

Her voice had a breathy quality to it that didn't conform at all with the casually offered invitation. It did, however, quite accurately reflect the present state of her nerves, which was somewhere between on end and shot. She'd been so certain Nick would use the betraying intensity of her response to ask the question he wanted answered, and for a moment there, she hadn't known what that answer would be.

"Dinner sounds good." He took another step back and jammed the hands that had been tangled in her hair only moments ago into his pockets. "Want me to bring anything?"

"Just Brian."

The desire still so evident in his eyes made his grin look almost wicked. "Safety in numbers?"

"Something like that," she mumbled with a smile.

"Chicken. What time do you want us?"

"What time is it now?"

His watch, one of those complicated things that could do everything but play the National Anthem, emerged from his sleeve. "Four."

"How about six, then?" That would give her two hours to regroup.

The second Nick left, Tory started to pace. She had to do something to calm herself down and get her perspective back. When the pacing didn't work, she grabbed her book from the table by the sofa. She could practice her deep-breathing exercises, and while she was doing them, she'd rehearse the little speech she wasn't at all convinced she wanted to deliver. Maybe she wouldn't have to. Maybe Nick had changed his mind. Maybe...

"Maybe you should concentrate on what you're doing," she muttered to herself an hour later. When the breathing techniques hadn't worked, she'd decided to try one of the stretching positions. Yoga had one thing going for it anyway. It was difficult to think about anything else when you were wobbling on one leg while trying to pull the other one behind your head.

Getting her foot behind her head was only a farfetched goal. Right now, she had it clasped at her waist and it didn't want to go any higher. Just one more inch.

Just as she pulled on her sock-covered foot, she heard the knock at her door—and promptly lost her balance. She landed in an ignominious heap on the rug in front of the sofa. "Come in," she called, and followed that up with a muttered "Damn" as she rubbed her hip. The stork position was going to take more work.

"Just wanted to tell you that Brian— What are you doing?"

Nick closed the door behind him, something between concern and laughter deepening the lines fanning from the corners of his eyes.

"What does it look like I'm doing?" She squinted at him, trying not to laugh. She could only imagine how totally graceless she must look at the moment.

Nick, on the other hand, looked wonderful. He had just tossed his jacket onto the peg by the door and turned around again. The powder-blue ski sweater he was wearing over a white turtleneck jersey made his tanned complexion appear even darker. And what that sweater did for his eyes, not to mention his chest, was indescribable.

Planting his hands at the waist of his jeans, he looked down at her. "Are you okay?"

"I'm fine. The only thing I wounded was my pride."

"Don't get up." The moment she started to do just that, he sat down on the carpet across from her. Picking up the book that had got her into her present position, he laid it between them. "Let's see what we've got here." The corners of his mouth tipped up. "I didn't know some of this stuff was physically possible."

"For some of us, it's not." She didn't want to be a stork anyway. "You're early."

"I know." He flipped another page. "I wanted to tell you that Brian ate a couple cans of chili when he went back to the tent, so he's not hungry. He said to thank you for the offer, though, and wants to know if he can have a rain check. Since your original invitation included both of us, I didn't know if you'd want me to stay. I saw Albert down at the inlet," he continued, taking one of his confusing subject leaps. "Sounds like you had a busy week."

Tory shook her head, both at the strange way his mind worked and at how comfortable he looked sitting there. He looked so... relaxed.

She leaned back against the sofa and crossed her legs at the ankles. If he could look relaxed, so could she—on the outside, anyway. "Tell Brian he can have the rain check. You can still stay for dinner, since Willy brought me a whole salmon and I need somebody to help me eat it. If you ran into Albert anywhere it would have to be at the inlet because the men are down there getting their boats ready to go seal hunting. And how do you know I had a busy week?" A glimmer of amusement danced in her eyes. "Did I miss anything?"

Nick chuckled and pushed the book aside to lean back on his hands. "You didn't miss a thing. I know you had a busy week because Albert said you'd used his radio to have some vaccine flown in. He mentioned that you ran out before you could get all the kids vaccinated at some kind of clinic you had a few days ago. That reminds me, come down to the tent tomorrow and I'll show you how to use our radio. It'll be a lot more convenient for you than having to walk to the village."

At her tentative nod, he continued. "And, let's see, while I was talking to Albert, one of the Rominoffs told me about the latest addition to their family, the baby you delivered last..." The arching of his eyebrows asked her to supply the information the new father apparently hadn't.

"Tuesday." She smiled, feeling considerably more at ease. There was no reason to be nervous when they were talking like this.

"Last Tuesday," he repeated, continuing with his present train of thought. "Then you spent most of Wednesday with Willy trying to get the puppy he adopted after Kai died to fetch the stick instead of running off to bury it. Wish I'd been there to see that."

She wished he had, too. "So, now that you know how I spent my time, tell me what you were doing."

Nick had told her about his work before—they'd actually had several conversations about it—and though Tory didn't understand the technicalities any better than he would have understood the procedure for an arterial graft, she sensed the deep satisfaction he'd found in his profession. He spoke easily, his eyes revealing the pleasure he took in her interest, and the deep resonance of his voice lulled her.

The man was a master at his art. And science was an art. He could find the precious bits of minerals and the power hidden beneath the earth's crust, then chip away at the layers until the wealth revealed itself. He had done that very same thing with her. Skillfully, patiently, he had drawn her out by unearthing what had lain buried for so long. He'd made her feel all the emotions she'd repressed. And he'd made her see what that elusive need she'd come here to find really was. It was simply a need to share and to love. She and her ex-husband had had their work in common, but they had never shared the way she and Nick could. The way they were doing now.

He concluded his comments and lifted himself to his feet. She had no idea what he'd been saying. He'd lost her somewhere between insulators and ice floes.

Now she watched while he walked over to where his jacket was hanging by the door. Extracting a small box from its pocket, he returned to sit down beside her on the colorful braid rug.

Balancing the box in the palm of his hand, he held it out to her. "I found this while we were spacing insulators."

The box was one of those foam things used to cushion specimen slides. Did he want to show her a slide of some mineral he'd discovered? Puzzled, she lifted the lid and felt her heart give an odd little lurch. Why had he brought her this?

There, in a handful of melting snow, was a tiny white flower. It was almost crystalline in its perfection, and its delicate petals were wrapped in a tight oval bud.

As if he had heard her unspoken question, he quietly said, "It reminded me of you."

Seven

Tory didn't know what to say, and Nick didn't give her a chance to formulate a response. "Watch this," he said, gently picking up the bud. "There were a bunch of these growing by some rocks, but this one was growing a few feet away in a patch of snow. When I picked it and held it in my hand, this happened."

Fascinated, bewildered, she blinked at the white petals slowly unfolding in the heat of his hand to reveal a center of orange and yellow as bright as the sun. Her throat felt tight. "That reminded you of me?"

He just smiled.

The petals began to close when he returned the flower to its cushion of snow, and he laid the box on the sofa behind them. Looking over at him, she knew she'd regret asking, but she couldn't stop herself. "Why?"

That made him hesitate. For several moments he just sat there studying the worn spot on the right knee of his jeans.

"When I first met you," he finally began, "you were just like that little snow flower. All wrapped up tight so no one could see the colors inside." Now that he was talking, all traces of hesitation vanished. Tipping her chin toward him, he held her eyes, and she was shaken by the absolute certainty she saw in his. "But there were times when I held you," he continued quietly, "that I could feel you opening up, and each time you tried to close back up again, some of the petals didn't quite fall back into place. When I filled that box with snow and watched the flower shut itself up when I put it inside, I guess I realized how fragile you are, how fragile it is, whatever you and I have."

He drew a deep breath, his gaze drifting over her face before he dropped his hand from her chin. "I know I'm saying this badly, Tory, but I'm trying to tell you that I don't want you to close up on me. If you want things to stay the way they are, then I'm not going to risk that happening by pushing you into something you don't want."

He might have thought his phrasing inadequate, but Tory had never heard anything more beautiful. He was telling her he cared. Really cared. Didn't he know what something like that did to a woman?

"You shouldn't do that," he scolded with that little half smile.

The tremulous breath she took brought with it the clean scent of the soap he'd used in the shower, the spicy after-shave he'd splashed on his cleanly shaven face. "I shouldn't do what?"

"Look at me that way."

She wasn't sure what her expression was, but something about it caused his chiseled features to tighten in forced self-control. He wanted to touch her. She was certain of that. But he'd curled his hand into a fist between them.

"You know something, Nick?" The muscle at the cleft in his chin bunched when she touched it with the tip of her finger. His whole jaw went rigid when she trailed that finger down to rest her hand at the base of his throat. She leaned forward. "I never have liked it when you tell me what to do."

Her kiss had begun with almost playful sweetness. Though Nick had barely moved, it started to intensify of its own accord. She had wanted to thank him for understanding, for his sensitivity, and for caring enough to bring her that precious flower. But the feel of his mouth softening beneath hers, the taste of him when her tongue teased his lips, elicited deeper reasons.

She wanted to express the love bursting in her heart and create the memories she would carry with her the rest of her life. If she couldn't have him forever, she could at least cherish whatever he was willing to give her now.

"Don't do this to me." He spoke the demand without conviction and cradled her in his arms. "It's hard enough wanting you without having you . . ."

"You already have me." Her words were muffled against his throat, the pulse there quickening when he heard her soft admission.

He allowed her lips to explore the texture of his skin below his jaw, her fingers to push through his hair and curve behind his head. Moving against her, he angled his head to meet her mouth once more.

The heat of his hand splaying over her ribs when he slipped it under her sweater, made her feel like the snow flower unfurling to seek the light. She leaned closer, needing more. It seemed to be a life-giving warmth, something so vital to her existence that she'd die without it.

The feeling intensified. His fingers burned a path beneath her breast, and a searing knot coiled deep inside when his palm pressed over its fullness. She could sense the way he was holding himself back, restraining that debilitating touch. All she could do was cling to him, encourage him with the movement of her mouth against his and pray that he wouldn't stop.

He didn't—not until long moments later when he'd lowered her to the floor and she arched toward him.

"Oh, Tory—" her name was an agonized plea "—I want you so much."

In bold response, she flattened her hand against his stomach.

He grasped her fingers, stilling their downward path. His voice was so thick she could barely hear it over the pulse pounding in her ears. "I can't take much more of this," he warned, his breathing ragged. "And in about two seconds, there won't be any going back."

It was taking everything he had to give her a chance to change her mind. The desire tensing his severely beautiful features quite effectively refuted his offer. It was a chance she didn't want anyway.

"I know." She sighed the words, glorying in the feel of his skin when she freed her hand and pushed it under his sweater. "I know."

The moan torn deep from within his chest vibrated against her lips. Conscious thought gave way to tactile sensations; rationality to a need that had its basis in the deepest part of her soul.

A trail of moist fire moved from her seeking mouth when he began to taste the soft skin at her throat. The heat building within her took the chill from the cool air when he lifted her, then pulled back to ease her sweater over her head and release the clasp of her bra to expose her breasts.

Easing her back down, he kept himself above her. With his finger he traced teasing circles around her dusky aureoles, seeming fascinated with their instinctive tightening. Through the veil of her lashes, she watched as he slowly lowered his head and his mouth covered one sensitized nipple. There was something about his expression that made him seem so vulnerable just then. That made her love him all the more.

Though Nick would never admit to needing anyone, at this moment he was silently saying he needed her. The tenderness of his touch, the rhythmic release and pull of his suckling, spoke of more than desire.

Threading her fingers through his hair, she pressed him to her. I love you! The words echoed in her mind, but the only sound that escaped was a strangled gasp when his tongue began a sensual descent down her stomach and his hand slipped over the fabric between her thighs. The motion he started there threatened to send the tightening knot that was building within uncoiling at any moment.

Then, his hand stilled. His leg had been thrown over hers, but the weight was no longer there. Before her body could decry that loss of contact, she felt his fingers working to unfasten the snap of her cords and heard the metallic rasp of a zipper.

"Lift your hips, Tory." His words seemed distant, muted by the huskiness in his deep voice.

Never before had she been so aware of her own body. Now it seemed to be responding to the most ordinary things. The roughness of the corduroy being slid down her legs and the silkiness of the bikinis that followed took on entirely different sensations. That same erotic roughness was repeated by his hand grazing along her calf, the sensation of the satiny nylon echoed when his hand gentled on the side of her hip.

She reached for him.

"Not yet," he whispered, catching her wrists. "Let me look at you."

There was hunger in his darkened eyes as he leaned forward to lay her hands beside her head. That hunger intensified when he brushed a strand of ebony hair from her flushed face and his gaze moved down to caress the alabaster smoothness of her breasts. Slowly his eyes drifted to the flatness of her stomach, then lingered on the downy triangle at the apex of her slender legs.

"Nick, please." So shaken was she by his unveiled admiration that her words were barely audible. "I need you."

"We need each other," he returned, finally allowing her trembling hands to draw away the unwanted barrier of his sweater.

The feel of his hard chest made the ache filling her every pore nearly unbearable. Where his motions had been steady and unhurried, her own seemed much less practiced when she worked his jeans over his hips. Nick didn't seem to mind. If anything, her more tentative touch appeared only to increase his desire for her.

With their clothing gone, Tory was dimly aware of the cool air enveloping them. The fire in the stove was burning low, but the fire in Nick's deliberately slow kiss provided all the warmth she needed. Nick was the fire. And she was the wind fanning the flame that threatened to consume them both.

The thrust of his tongue into the sweetness of her mouth and its agonizingly slow withdrawal was a sensual prelude to the moments that followed. It wasn't until her caresses became more urgent, more demanding, that she felt his control begin to slip. Her fingers dug into the firm flesh of his hips, coaxing him to align himself more intimately. He needed no more encouragement than that. She felt his fingers drift along the underside of her thigh, their insistent pressure opening her to him. The welcomed weight of his body settled fully upon her. Arching upward, she brought him to her and felt the smooth muscles in his back coil with the tension of the gentle pace he set. Then the pace quickened. Urgency joined tenderness. She knew he couldn't make it last any longer.

Tory had been hanging on the edges of reality. But Nick led her to a place beyond confinement. He hurled her toward it, waiting until she entered that world where substance no longer existed, then joined her there, leaving them both suspended.

Slowly, inevitably, came their descent from that place. They returned to the sounds of the embers settling in the stove, and the wind moaning against the side of the cabin as they lay wrapped in each other's arms on the colorful braid rug.

The room seemed considerably cooler than it had only a few moments before. It didn't matter, though. Nick's body felt damp and deliciously warm. A contentment unlike anything she'd ever known filled her, making little things like goose bumps completely inconsequential. All that did matter was Nick, and she wished there was some way she could tell him how utterly peaceful she felt.

He must have mistaken the reason for her silence. Pulling his arm from beneath her head, he pulled his weight to his elbows and smoothed away the strands of hair clinging to her forehead. There was such tenderness in his touch and such relief in his eyes when he saw her languorous smile. "No regrets?" he asked with gentle concern.

"None," she sighed, and saw something that looked very much like regret creeping into his expression. "Do you have any?"

"Just one." Seeing consternation rapidly replacing contentment, he gave her a slightly lopsided smile and dropped a kiss on the tip of her nose. "A few weeks ago, a year seemed like a long time." The way his eyes caressed her face was as potent as the feel of his hand drifting down her side. "Now it doesn't seem anywhere near long enough."

She knew exactly what he meant.

The weeks sped by, making even the days when Nick was gone seem more like a dream than reality. Tory held clinics two days a week and spent every Monday making rounds to check up on the elderly villagers who couldn't make it to her cabin. Nick's men demanded little attention, and she found a comfortable balance between her work and the projects she'd set out to tackle for herself. Nick didn't interrupt her routine anywhere near often enough, though. It was only when he would return to camp ahead of his crew or show up with the excuse that he'd come back for supplies that they were able to find time alone together.

It was those hours she wished she could harness, slow down somehow so the present wouldn't become the past. The memories he was helping her create were the stuff of fantasies, and she was convinced she was as close to heaven as a mere mortal could come. But time stood still for no one. Spring had finally melted into summer.

Summer was a relative term. Fifty degrees and patches of blue sky vying for space among the billowy gray and white clouds was as close to that season as it ever got here.

Sitting on a smooth rock next to the pile of driftwood she and Nick had just collected, Tory leaned back on her hands and watched him walk to the shore a few yards away. He pushed his hands into his pockets, lifting his head so the breeze could blow the thick, dark blond hair from his forehead.

She wondered what he was thinking about, and a soft smile curved her lips. Trying to figure out Nick's thoughts was like trying to read an X ray when half the bulbs on the viewing screen were blown out. You couldn't ever quite get the whole picture. Sometimes she felt she knew him so well, but more often she felt she didn't know him at all. There was an elusiveness about him, something she wanted desperately to discover but knew he'd never allow her to. He never talked about the future and seldom questioned the past. It was as if nothing existed for him beyond the present, and the present was all he needed.

Tory tried to be content with that, too. But it was hard, because she wanted so much more.

Leaning forward, she hugged her arms over her heavy teal sweater and rested her elbows on the knees of her jeans. Funny how much pleasure she found simply watching him. He looked so much a part of his surroundings, as though this was the only place on earth he truly belonged. She tried to picture him in slacks and a sport coat, standing behind a lectern while he conducted one of the classes he used to teach. The image refused to form. All she could visualize was what she was seeing now.

The down vest he wore over his flannel shirt was open. With his hands in his pockets, the sides were held back, making his narrow hips look even leaner. He'd rolled his shirt sleeves back to expose the dark brown hair swirling over his powerful forearms, and the length of his long legs gave him the stance of a man in command of himself and all he surveyed. She couldn't see his face, but she didn't have to. Every plane and angle had been committed to memory. If she had to guess at his expression, she was sure it would be as enigmatic as always.

It was.

"This place is incredible," he said, his easy, effortless gait bringing him to stand in front of her.

She smiled. "Indescribable is more like it."

"Better be careful." A familiar note of teasing tempered his warning. "You talk like that, somebody might think you're letting this place get to you."

This place wasn't all that had got to her.

Moving over so he could sit down on her rock, she lifted her face to the salt-tanged breeze. "I don't think it's a matter of letting it happen," she explained, her tone wistful. "It just gets to you all by itself without giving you any choice in the matter. There's no sense fighting it because it's going to leave its mark no matter what you do." Her eyes narrowed on the rocky shoal several hundred feet out from the shoreline. "It's a gift, and the best thing to do with something like this is just to enjoy it."

He sent a thoughtful glance skipping over her serene features. "I've got the feeling I missed something. Are we talking about the same thing?"

His ability to read between her mental lines was terribly unnerving. The description she'd just given of how the rugged splendor of the island affected her was also a fairly accurate recital of how she felt about him.

"Of course we're talking about the same thing." Her defense was softened by the lilt in her voice. "We're talking about that ocean—" she inclined her head toward the surf rolling up the rock-strewn beach "—and that sky, and that little island." Motioning toward the shoal that had held her attention a moment ago, she prepared to continue her inventory. But instead of pointing out the topography Nick was already quite familiar with, she opted to satisfy her curiosity. The look he was giving her said she'd made her point anyway. "Are those seals?"

The shoal was alive with the glistening fur of sea mammals undulating their way across the foamy gray-green surf. The sound of their muted grunts and barks had been so much a part of the roaring ocean and the wind whistling through the tall grass behind her that she hadn't really noticed the noise until now.

Nick gave his head a negative shake and the corner of his mouth twitched. "They're sea lions. There's a breeding colony over on Bogoslof Island. Guess things got a little busy over there, so these guys came over for a little R & R."

She wasn't going to touch that one, though it was obvious from the devilish glint in Nick's eyes that he expected her to. No sense being predictable.

She turned her grin to the toes of her boots.

With an exaggerated sigh, he caught her hand and pulled her to her feet. "Since you didn't bite on that one, let's walk down to the inlet and watch the birds." His brows jiggled in a playful leer. "Maybe I can trap you in a discussion about the illicit mating practices of puffins."

Trying to look scandalized wasn't easy when you wanted to laugh. Nick was clearly in one of his less-than-serious moods. "Those birds are so adorable I can't imagine anything about them being illicit." The birds he was talking about looked like little clowns to her, with their black bodies, huge orange beaks and the silly yellow plumes that hung over their white masks.

"How about something that's definitely not adorable? Like the wanton walrus?"

"Oh, Nick. That was awful."

"The sex life of the sea urchin?" he prodded, hopeful. "Now there's a prickly subject for you."

She buried her groan in the front of his shirt. "I think all this salt air is corroding your brain."

The teasing slipped from his eyes when he pressed his hand to the small of her back, bringing her closer. "It's got nothing to do with the air, honey."

There was no mistaking his message. She could feel him, and that made her even more aware of the feminine power she wielded. The fact that he held the counterpart to that power was something he had to know.

"I think we'd better go for that walk," was her way of saying that if they stood here any longer looking at each other like this, they'd probably wind up offending the sensibilities of the sea lions.

His husky "Good idea" ended in a throaty chuckle. Hugging her to his side, he steered her over a blob of seaweed and started down the shore. "Let's go get a crab pot and see if we can catch something for dinner. I'm in the mood for crab and homemade bread."

"Just where are you going to get this 'homemade bread'?" she inquired, matching her strides to his.

"I thought you'd make it."

"Fat chance. Last time I tried it, Willy and I wound up feeding it to the puffins."

Nick responded with a look of sudden insight. "So that's why the flock was rolling around on the beach. They were all suffering from indigestion."

"You're not making any points, Spencer. There's a knack to baking I just haven't quite mastered yet. And since I recognize my limitations in the domestic department, I can't see any sense wasting my flour on bird food. If you want something with your crab, it'll have to be crackers."

Without breaking stride, he dropped a kiss on the tip of her nose. "You know what I really miss?" he asked. "I miss hot apple pie. How about you?"

She was becoming quite adept at filling in his verbal blanks. Making a mental note to talk to Katrina about how to build a piecrust and to ask Albert to pick up some apples for her the next time he went to the store in Dutch, she responded with a simple, "Oranges."

"Nothing else?"

Surprisingly enough, there really wasn't much else she missed about her "other life," as she'd come to think of it. Well, maybe she missed her automatic dishwasher a little, but that didn't seem worth mentioning. "Not really. Just oranges."

"Well, it won't be long before you have them again." Some of the lightness left his tone. "There's plenty of them in California." Kicking at a shell, he slanted her a curiously hesitant glance, then looked away. "What are you going to do when you go back?"

Tory's pace faltered, but she picked it up again in a deliberate attempt to quell the sinking feeling in the pit of her stomach. Why did he have to bring that up now? She didn't want to think about going back. When she did that, she was all too aware of how quickly the next several months were going to pass.

"I'm not sure," she hedged, and tried to change the subject. "We forgot the firewood. Let's take it up to the cabin and then go get the—"

"It'll be there when we get back," he interrupted, shoving her hand into the pocket of his vest with his own. "Are you going back to the hospital in L.A.?"

Her sigh of resignation was as soft as the wind scattering strands of gleaming black hair across her cheeks. When Nick honed in on something, there was no way to budge him from his chosen topic. She hadn't quite figured out how that particular trait fit with the one that made it so easy for him to skip from one subject to another without seeming to miss anything in between.

"I'm not going back to California." She followed him up and over a log that some long-ago wave had put in their path. Since he had possession of her hand, she couldn't very well go around it. "There're a few places in New England that are practically begging for doctors. Maybe I'll start a practice in a fishing village in Maine."

Her tone made her words sound frivolous, but they weren't. Though she hadn't given the idea a whole lot of thought, the seed had planted itself in her mind a few weeks ago. It seemed to have taken a pretty firm root.

Nick looked skeptical and oddly pleased. "Why?"

She shrugged. "I suppose a lot of it has to do with what we were talking about before. After you've lived in a place like this, it's hard to imagine going back to a city. I don't know what it is exactly. Sort of a..." Her voice trailed off when she was unable to put words to what was more of a feeling than anything else.

Nick squeezed her hand. "I know what you mean. I've tried to explain it before, but I can't, either. Why Maine?"

"Because I think it might be a little like this."

"It's nothing like this," he chuckled. "Have you ever been there?"

She admitted that she hadn't. "I've just read about it. Have you?" And why, she wondered, are you grinning like that?

She got her answers as soon as they'd negotiated the small tidal pool that had sprung up in front of them. "That's where I used to teach. I've got a house outside Portland that I rent out while I'm gone, which is usually most of the time."

It was her turn to look puzzled, only she meant that look for herself. He'd never mentioned this before. Of all the places she could think of going, why had it turned out to be Maine?

Nick didn't see her expression. He was watching a flock of white-winged Ptarmigans take flight at their approach. "If you do decide to move there, let me know. I'll look you up when I get back."

Look her up? Tory used the excuse of watching where she was going to avoid looking at him. He'd sounded so casual, so... uncommitted.

Which is exactly how he told you he feels about relationships, she reminded herself, and tried to seem interested when he started pointing out the striation one of the recent tremors had revealed above the bank by relocating a few thousand tons of rock.

The Aleutians sat atop one of the most active faults in the world. Tory had felt only a few of those minor rumblings, but now she felt as precarious as the boulder Nick was indicating. It sat balanced on a much smaller one, and it wouldn't take much to send it crashing into the ocean beating in the cove beneath it. Likewise, she knew it wouldn't take much for her to start feeling the hurt that comes from loving someone who so obviously doesn't love you. Nick cared for her. She knew that. But she also knew there was no place for her in his life beyond the present.

A dull ache centered in her chest, and she fell silent.

Either Nick didn't notice how quiet she'd become or he was deliberately filling what was usually a comfortable silence with conversation that had become quite one-sided. They'd reached the path leading from the shore to Albert's cabin, where they were going to borrow the crab pot. Rather than starting up the winding path, Nick swung himself in front of her and stopped. He'd apparently been very aware of her silence.

"I'd offer you a penny for them," he said quietly. "But they're worth a lot more than that to me." The intensity in his eyes searching her upturned face was as powerful as the ocean booming against the craggy rocks behind her. "Tell me what's wrong."

Everything. "Nothing," she whispered, and tried to smile. She could tell he didn't believe her. The way she'd just looked away probably had something to do with it.

Tipping her chin up with his finger, he coaxed her head back toward him. "Don't close up on me, Tory. Ever since I brought up your going back, you ..." He closed his eyes, swallowing his words with a self-deprecating breath. "Oh, honey," he sighed, gathering her in his arms. "I'm sorry. I don't like to think about it, either, but there're some things about you I just need to know—and some things I'm almost afraid to ask."

The regret he felt at having so unwittingly hurt her was in his embrace. There was something else there, too—a kind of longing that went far beyond anything she'd felt in him before. It seemed as tangible as his hard length seeking her softer curves and the warmth of his lips moving against her own.

The ache she'd been so busily telling herself she didn't feel vaporized beneath the gentle persuasion of his mouth. He'd been only partly right when he'd guessed the reason for her too-revealing withdrawal. But he'd also comforted her by admitting that she meant more to him than he'd ever said and that he, too, recognized how precious their time together was. But what was it he was afraid to ask?

It felt as though her heart was beating in her throat when he lifted his head to smile down at her. Anticipation joined all the other things she felt whenever he held her. Did he want her to stay? Was that it? Could he possibly. . . ?

She interrupted her mental questions with a verbal one when he tucked her against his side and started back toward the shore. "Where are we going?"

"Back to get the firewood," he returned with that familiar determined set to his jaw. "The guys went fishing today, so we'll just have whatever they caught for dinner."

The huskiness in his voice told her he had more than dinner on his mind. At the moment, so did she. But she was fairly certain their thoughts weren't running in the same direction. Nick hadn't said he was afraid to ask something *of* her. It was something *about* her.

"Nick?" His pace was much quicker than the one he'd set to bring them here and she tried to keep up with his long-legged strides. "You said there was something you were afraid to ask me." Her reminder did nothing but slacken his pace a little. Since it didn't look as if he was going to say anything, she ventured further. "You know I'll tell you whatever you want to—"

The clenching of his jaw stopped her before his words did. "I don't think I want to hear," he all but growled.

"Wait a minute!" She came to a halt. Nick reluctantly stopped with her. "What is it you want to know anyway?" She hardly had any ghastly secrets to reveal and couldn't begin to imagine what was causing him to look so tense all of a sudden.

Grabbing her hand, he pulled her back into step. It wasn't until they'd covered a good two hundred feet that he finally muttered, "Your ex-husband." He expanded on that two steps later. "What happened?"

A mask of reticence shadowed his rough-hewn features. There was something in that look that reminded her of the volatile forces hidden beneath the land he was so determined to trap and tame. Explosive, vital, Nick was very much like his land. She had the feeling that what was hidden behind his stony expression now was nothing but plain old jealousy. The tightness in his voice was about the most wonderful thing she'd ever heard.

It was very hard not to smile. "We just had too many differences," she began easily, and watched his jaw relax while she explained about her marriage to the eminent Dr. Keith Richards. What she had thought was love had turned out to be only admiration. Admiration that had quickly turned to disillusionment when she'd discovered that Keith hadn't cared about her so much as about what he thought he could make of her—the perfect doctor, the perfect wife, the perfect hostess. Tory was too human to be perfect.

By the time she and Nick reached the spot they'd started out from, Nick had a pretty clear picture. He released her hand and picked up several pieces of the driftwood they'd collected earlier. Tory held out her hands so he could stack them in her arms. "For what it's worth, I like you just the way you are, warts and all."

That was worth a lot. "I don't have any warts!"

"Maybe not. But you do have a cute little mole on your—"

The mole was on her left hip, but Nick didn't have a chance to remind her of its location before Brian's booming "There you guys are!" cut him off. "I've been looking all over for you." Jogging the last few yards through the knee-deep, sea-misted grass, he planted himself in front of Tory. "Craig radioed over a couple of hours ago. He said it's nothing urgent, but he wants you to call him back as soon as you can."

Brian didn't have any more information than that. Nick didn't seem to know what was going on, either. The questioning glance she tossed at him earned her nothing but a shrug.

Why would Craig be calling her?

Eight

When Nick first asked Tory to take over Craig's medical duties, she'd made it clear that medical attention was absolutely all she was going to provide. That little exercise in self-assertion had been long since forgotten. Tonight she had provided the cornmeal for the fish Dean fried, the dishes Spike washed and left to be dried and the coffee everyone, including Nick, was drinking now. She'd even provided the present topic of conversation by asking why Mike hadn't come for dinner and why he'd chosen to spend his day off in the tent instead of going fishing with the other guys.

His excuse for not joining them this time, according to Brian, was the need to work on some equipment Spike insisted was already in perfect working order.

Mike's increasing withdrawal had been an indirect reason for Craig's call to her earlier that afternoon.

The behavioral study he'd been conducting—and would still be conducting if he'd been here instead of in therapy over in Anchorage—was already behind schedule. He'd been so certain he'd be back here by now, but because it would be a few more weeks before he could return, he wanted Tory's help. He needed her observations about how the crew interacted with one another, and he wanted her to talk to Dean about the blowout between the two men Nick had fired.

Tory had been fascinated when Craig had gone on to explain his theory about how the physical changes that take place in the body when it was subjected to long periods of cold affected emotions and the thinking process. She was more than willing to start the tests he wanted and had told him so. He must have known she'd offer. The additional equipment she'd need was already on its way.

"I'm surprised he didn't ask for your help sooner," was all Nick had said when she'd told him what Craig wanted. But the uneasy glance he'd tossed her had considerably dampened her enthusiasm.

It was the way Nick had looked at her then, and the wariness in his expression as he watched her now, that was making it difficult to concentrate on the men's conversation.

"...Not saying much," Brian was saying about their absent crew member, "but I think it's got something to do with the letter he got from his girlfriend a couple weeks ago." He glanced from Dean and Nick, lounging at opposite ends of the sofa, to Spike, who was sitting on a stool with his back propped against the wall. "She wants him to come home so they can get married, but he's signed up for the duration and isn't sure he wants to give this up."

From where Tory was sitting next to Brian at the noxious-pink counter, she saw Nick surreptitiously shake his head. It was as if he was trying to tell Brian to be quiet, but she was the only one who caught that silent admonition.

"He cares about her," Brian continued, "but he cares about his work, too. From what little he's said, I get the feeling she's the clinging-vine type."

Dean had a knowing look on his now healed face. "That's the last thing he needs. It takes a special kind of woman to marry the likes of us. Like my Anna. Strong and independent. Somebody who's got a life of her own but doesn't mind havin' her life interrupted by a husband who pops in for a few months every year or so. A clingin' vine won't cut it."

"Sometimes it doesn't work with the independent type, either," Brian observed with a wry smile. "Linda and I only lasted five years, but in our profession, I guess even that's something of a record."

Spike muttered something about avoiding the whole mess in the first place. Nick just stared down at the cup he held suspended between his knees.

"Have you talked to Mike about this?" Dean asked Nick, and Tory felt an uncomfortable knot form in her stomach when Nick's jaw gave a telling jerk.

"I tried," Nick said, looking everywhere but at Tory. "He didn't like what I had to say."

Without quite knowing why, Tory had the feeling she wouldn't like whatever he'd said, either. She bit her lip rather than ask him to elaborate.

Before her teeth drew blood, Spike voiced that question for her. "What did you say?"

This time Nick did look at her. That glance was brief and definitely guarded. It didn't seem as though he wanted to answer, but he didn't have much choice.

"I just told him about the number of marriages I've seen break up because of the enforced absences these types of expeditions demand," he explained, directing his words to the braided rug beneath his feet. "If he wants to get married, he might as well forget about this kind of work. On the other hand, if he wants to stay here or hook up with another team like this in the future, he might as well forget about marriage." Drawing a deep breath, he lifted his cup. Then, apparently deciding he didn't want the coffee, he lowered it again. "Whatever he does, he's going to have to make up his mind soon, before I have to make the decision for him."

Dean scowled. "What d'ya mean?"

"I mean that if he doesn't shape up, I'm going to send him back. He's getting so preoccupied that his work is suffering, and I can't have that. Some of what we do is too dangerous..."

Tory didn't hear what Nick was saying. All she heard was the dull thud of her heart pounding in the hollow of her chest. The emotional roller coaster she'd been riding all day had just taken another plunge. She'd been blissfully happy just being with Nick until he'd mentioned her leaving while they'd been on the beach and made that comment about "looking her up." Then the ache brought on by his seemingly cavalier attitude about their relationship had been banished quite effectively when he'd let her see how much she meant to him. Now it was painfully clear that she didn't mean enough.

Though she'd known all along how he felt about marriage, there was something about actually hearing him confirm it that brought that ache back with a vengeance. Telling herself she'd known what she was getting into didn't help a bit. Neither did trying to

convince herself that she hadn't wanted marriage in
the first place.

No one in that room could possibly have known the
effort it took to plaster the smile on her face when she
walked over to the stove and picked up the pot. "More
coffee, anyone?"

She hadn't meant to look at Nick, but his were the
first pair of eyes she encountered when she turned
around with the blue enameled pot in her hand. The
disquiet in his eyes had compounded itself, but the rest
of his features were remarkably bland. From the relaxed postures of the other men as they accepted or
declined her offer of coffee, none of them appeared to
notice the subtle tension beginning to fill the atmos-
phere.

The previous topic of conversation had faded. For
that, Tory was exceedingly grateful. But the one Dean
introduced right after he'd groaned something about
having eaten too much seemed to explain why Nick
had been acting so strangely ever since she'd told him
about Craig's call.

"With Craig comin' back," he drawled, stretching,
"ya'll think we'll be movin' the base over to Umnak
pretty soon?"

Nick didn't answer. His response was to run his
hand over his face and shoot the big Texan a look that
clearly said, *Why in the hell did you have to bring that
up?*

Forcing her grip to relax rather than tighten on the
handle of the coffeepot when she set it back on the
stove, Tory made her tone much lighter than it wanted
to be. "I didn't know you were thinking about moving the base."

"We've been talkin' about it ever since we got
here," Dean chuckled, oblivious to the effort it was

taking for Tory to appear nothing more than mildly interested. "All we've been waitin' for is for Craig to get back. He'll be bringin' the two replacements, so we'll have a full crew again. And since the base was supposed to be over there anyway, we might as well move it."

Spike leaned forward, scratching the fuzzy rim of beige-brown hair below his bald spot. "We found potential here, too."

Dean's nod indicated agreement, but he was reluctant to abandon his position. "We spend most of our time over on Umnak and Chuginadak, though. That's okay while the weather holds, but what about a couple months from now when it starts snowin' again?" Cupping his hands behind his head, he angled himself on the sofa when Nick stood up. "So, what about it, boss?"

Nick's level gaze included everyone except Tory. "I'm still thinking about it," he muttered, and leaned against the wall next to Spike. "It probably wouldn't hurt to concentrate on the area around here for the next few weeks instead of going back to one of the other islands tomorrow. With Tory helping Craig out with his study, she'll need you guys around anyway."

"Sounds like a plan." Dean stretched again and stifled a yawn. "We can finish everything up here, then we won't have to come back after we relocate the base."

Two pairs of eyes—narrowly slitted turquoise ones and Brian's—had settled on Tory, specifically on her hands, which were strangling her cup. Leaning toward her, Brian whispered, "You're going to break it," then glanced over at Nick. When he pulled back again, he seemed to have caught a glimpse of the strain that was somehow escaping the others' notice.

"We'll talk about this later," Nick informed his men. "No need to bore Tory any more than we have already."

Tory was far from bored. And it was obvious from his forced smile that Nick knew it.

Brian caught his boss's uneasiness, along with the stress that made Tory's smile look even weaker than it felt. "Yeah, come on, you guys, let's give the girl a break." Giving her what seemed like an awfully sympathetic pat on the arm as he stood up, he walked over to pull an armful of jackets from the pegs by the door. "Let's get out of here and see if we can't get Mike interested in a poker game."

Dean seemed to consider Brian's suggestion while he lifted his considerable bulk from the sofa. "Might not be a bad idea." Giving Tory a grin as wide as Texas, he added, "Sure would hate to wear out our welcome. I keep forgettin' how much we've been imposin' on you. Wanna try to win back the five bucks ya'll lost last week, Nick?"

The men hadn't been imposing at all. She loved their company and the way they'd so easily accepted her as a member of their team. She didn't get a chance to tell Dean that, though. Brian had taken it upon himself to respond to the question Dean had just posed.

"Nick has to stay and dry dishes."

Spike slid off his stool. "I'll do 'em."

"I'll help." Dean stepped forward.

"No, you don't." Brian grabbed Spike's arm and shoved a jacket into Dean's stomach. "We cleared and washed. K.P. gets an even split. Since Tory helped Dean with the cooking, the boss man has to dry."

Neither man seemed interested in upsetting the K.P. roster, though they were the only two who didn't know what Brian was trying to do. Nick certainly could tell what was going on. His expression was somewhere between a sincere "Thank you" and a dry "Thanks a lot" when Brian followed Spike and Dean out the door.

For several very long seconds Tory stood staring at the arm of the brown tweed sofa. Crossing her arms— a gesture she knew he hated, but one she couldn't help at the moment—she ventured a sideways glance in Nick's direction.

His hands were clasped between his knees, his gaze intent on the blues and browns and reds plaited in the rug. The kerosene lamp burning on the table beside him yellowed those colors, but its light shot slivers of liquid silver through his golden-brown hair. It didn't do a thing, however, to soften the defensive set of his mouth.

Sounding only slightly less guarded than he looked, he finally broke the ear-splitting quiet. "I wasn't going to say anything about moving the base until after Craig got here."

It came as no surprise that he'd known exactly what she was thinking about. "Why not?"

"Because I couldn't see any point in talking about something that might not happen."

"You mean you might stay here?" she inquired as casually as possible.

It was either the deceptive calm in her voice or the fact that he'd just noticed her arms that worked his forehead into a frown. "And we might not."

If anyone had asked her to describe Nicholas Spencer at that precise moment, she could have done it in one all-encompassing word: ambiguous! There was the distinct possibility that the word had been invented for him in the first place.

Her nails threatened to punch right through the weave of her teal-colored sweater. It was all she could do to keep from demanding an answer to the question screaming in her head. He knew how short their time together would be. But it looked as though even that time was going to be taken from her—by him! Just how long do we have, anyway? she wanted to know. Eight months? Two? A week? Maybe we should just get it all over with right now!

Closing her eyes, she drew a stabilizing breath. Getting irrational wouldn't solve anything. It was only that part of her that didn't want to feel the hurt that was making her think like this. The hurt was inevitable, though. She'd opened herself up to it just as she'd opened herself up to all the other things Nick had made her feel again.

Old habits die hard sometimes, and she hastily pieced back a few of the bricks that had crumbled. Or she tried to. "Why don't you go join the poker game?" she suggested with a smile that didn't quite work. "I'll give you a break from K.P. if you promise not to tell the guys you didn't dry the dishes."

Before she could even complete the step she'd taken toward the counter, Nick was in front of her. His hands curved over her shoulders, drawing her against him so sharply that her head snapped back.

"Don't do that!" The harsh command was tempered with the underlying plea in his deep voice. "Talk to me," he urged more quietly.

His touch had gentled, and the feel of his hands slipping across her back to hold her against him was almost more than she could handle. No matter how desperately she wanted to resurrect her old barriers, Nick would never let her. When he held her like this—as though she was as precious and as vital to him as the

very air he breathed—it was so hard for her to remember to keep her feelings in check.

"I don't want you to go." Her admission was faint,
muffled as it was against the soft flannel of his shirt.
But Nick heard.

"Oh, honey," he sighed, stroking her hair as he
breathed in the clean scent of baby shampoo clinging
to the midnight tresses that now touched her shoulders. "Didn't it ever occur to you that I don't *want* to
leave?"

He must not have expected an answer. The pressure
of his cheek grazing hers lifted her head from his
chest. A moment later his lips were moving over her
mouth.

The trembling seemed to start in her feet. It was a
disconcerting vibration that had nothing at all to do
with the longing in Nick's kiss. It was more of a disorienting shudder, accompanied by the rattling of
dishes skittering along the counter and crashing to the
floor. The plank boards seemed to tip and sway with
a rolling motion that might have been gentle if it
hadn't been for the sudden lurch that made Nick grab
for the counter before he shoved her away.

Over the creaking groan of the walls and the rumbling that seemed to be coming from everywhere, she
heard Nick's tight "Get in the doorway!"

That was exactly where she was headed. Anyone
who had lived in California knew about earth-
quakes—and this felt infinitely more threatening than
the faint tremors she'd noticed during the past few
weeks.

Her hand slapped against the frame as she jerked
the door open. Nick darted behind her, heading toward the sofa. An instant later, the room was plunged
into darkness. Something heavy hit the table by the

sofa and she heard Nick voice a terse "Damn" just before his arm bumped her side.

Tory could cope with blizzards and the gale-force winds she'd sometimes fought to get to her patients, but this exhibition of nature's power was something that terrified her. It gave a whole new meaning to "insecurity."

Grabbing the only solid thing she could find— Nick—she clung to him in the open doorway while the Aleutian Trench underwent a subtle, if not exactly inaudible, arrangement of its two major tectonic plates.

Forty-five seconds that seemed more like forty-five years later, the only thing still shaking was Tory.

"Are you okay?" came Nick's soft inquiry when he pried her arms from around his waist.

"I think so," she lied into the darkness, and felt him move away from her.

Turning around when he stepped aside, she slid her back along the door frame to sit on the threshold. Somehow he'd had the presence of mind to blow out the lamps before he joined her at the door—a fire was the last thing they needed—and everything was pitch black.

She squinted into the dark. "Where are you?"

"I think I'm in the kitchen. Nope. Wrong side of the counter. Where're the matches?"

"I-In the drawer by the sink."

"You sound a little shaky," he observed with what was probably in irritatingly calm smile.

Of course she sounded shaky! How else was she supposed to sound when every cell in her body was vibrating?

The metallic clank of the stove handle being lifted punched through a quiet bordering on eerie. A moment later the fire burning inside had illuminated the room enough for Nick to find what he was looking for.

Reaching for the lamp he'd carried to the counter, he struck a match and touched it to the wick. "We might get a couple of aftershocks. If one hits before I get back—" he flipped the match into the stove and kicked the metal door closed with his booted foot "—blow this thing out and get back in the doorway."

"Where are you going?" She knew the panic in her voice was evident, but frankly didn't much care.

"Down to the tent. I'll be right back."

"I'm coming with you." An aftershock was something she had no intention of riding out alone.

Nick must have realized there was no sense arguing with her. Slipping his arm around her waist, he pulled her to her feet, took her the three steps to the counter to blow the lamp out again and led her cautiously around the side of the cabin.

They didn't have to go very far. Just before they reached the little hill separating her cabin from the camp, Brian and Spike came running toward them with a flashlight so bright it would have made a car's headlights look dim. Another arc of white light swept the ground behind them. Mike and Dean were fast on their heels.

Tory was absolutely certain the earthquake must have jarred something loose in their brains. Instead of looking anxious or afraid or even mildly concerned, all the men were grinning.

Her eyes darted to Nick, his features clearly visible in the light bouncing off his chest. He was grinning, too!

It didn't take long to figure out why. Dean couldn't wait to check the readings to see how strong the tremor had been. "Probably only about two point five or a three," he noted, then asked if anyone wanted to take bets to see if he was right.

Even Mike looked excited, which was nice to see for a change. Spike and Brian were babbling about ground shift. And Nick had stepped right into the middle of a conversation that sounded like Greek to her.

None of the men seemed to notice the way she kept glancing nervously from them to the ground. They didn't seem to notice her at all—until an aftershock hit. It was only a faint, barely negligible repetition of the tremor that had preceded it, but it was enough to send her lurching toward the man she was closest to— which just happened to be Dean.

"Just another baby one," Mike muttered, sounding quite disappointed when the rumbling stopped within a few seconds.

"Might as well get back to the poker game," said Dean, placing a brotherly pat on the white-knuckled fingers biting into his forearm. "Want to stay in the tent with us tonight, Tory? I can hang a blanket around my cot for you, if ya'd like."

She was giving serious thought to the offer when she felt Nick's arm curve around her waist and its gentle pressure pulling her to his side. "I'll stay with her," Nick replied, openly hugging her against him.

Three sets of eyebrows arched in unison at the possessiveness in their boss's voice, not to mention the very proprietary way he was holding her. The only brows that hadn't snapped up were Brian's. All he did was smile.

"Unless something happens in the meantime," Nick continued easily, "I'll see you guys in the morning."

It was amid a considerable amount of throat clearing and mumbled good-nights that the flashlight beams arched and the men followed them back to their camp.

"I don't understand it," Tory mused in a voice that wasn't quite as strong as usual when she and Nick started picking their way back around her cabin. "They all acted like it was fun."

"Like what was?"

"The earthquake!"

"That was just a little tremor, Tory."

"That's your opinion. Weren't you even a little nervous? You weren't even shaking." She'd made her observation sound like an accusation.

"Sure I was," he chuckled. "You just couldn't tell because you and everything else was, too."

She smiled into the now quiet night, but the smile quickly faded. "Nick?"

"Hmm?" He stepped through the door, pulling her in behind him.

"Maybe I should just sleep on Dean's cot."

Though she couldn't see a thing, she was certain the "Why?" she heard was accompanied by a frown.

"Because of what your men will think if you spend the night here."

"And what," he inquired in the tone of someone who is already well aware of the answer, "is that?"

"Oh, come on, Nick. You know what I mean. The guys all—"

"The guys all think you're wonderful," he interrupted, and circling her waist with his arms, leaned against the counter. "Not one of them is going to think any less of you or me because we happened to have found something pretty special for ourselves. Neither one of us wants to flaunt what we have in their faces, but tonight I just happen to have the perfect excuse for being with you. Since that doesn't happen anywhere near often enough..."

His head had bent so that his words rushed softly against her ear. It was the feel of his lips moving down the side of her neck and the heat of his hand slipping beneath her sweater that made her forget the hesitation she'd felt only a moment ago. Nick was right. "What are you doing?"

"I'm trying to make you forget about things like my men and earthquakes."

"I thought you said it was only a tremor."

"So I did," he whispered, covering the soft swell of her breast with his palm only an instant before his tongue demanded entrance into the sweet softness of her mouth.

There was a lot to be said for his diversionary tactics.

When she'd felt the shudderings of the earth, Tory had promised herself not to waste a single second worrying about the future. There were forces beyond both her and Nick that could take them from each other and leave them no choice as to when that might happen. Nick wanted her. She loved him. For now, that was all that mattered.

The only tremors Tory felt for the rest of that night were the ones Nick caused to register on her own internal Richter scale.

The men were busier than ever during the weeks preceding Craig's return. So was Tory. Between her biweekly clinics, the trips to the villagers who couldn't make it to those clinics and all the reading material Craig had sent, she had time for little else. The only free time anyone had was in the evening. Since the crew members spent most of those evenings at Tory's engaged in lively discussions about all the new data they were collecting, she and Nick were rarely alone. Because of his position as head of the expedition, and to avoid any potential morale problems, Nick spent his nights in the tent. Tory spent most of hers staring at the new cracks the tremors had left in the ceiling above her bed.

The quake hadn't caused any damage in the village, but it had changed the shape of a few islands farther along the chain. Tory had swallowed her sigh of relief when one of the men mentioned that the site for the base on Umnak wasn't there anymore. There was a lot of talk about finding another site. Most of it, though, was interspersed with teasing comments about how much time Nick would waste flying back and forth to see Tory.

She accepted the good-natured banter with the same good grace she was showing Craig now. He'd arrived yesterday and had waited only long enough to say hello to the men before searching her out. He was clearly bent on making up for lost time.

At the moment, he was sitting on one of the stools. Nick was leaning against the counter next to him, his long legs crossed negligently at the ankles. They were waiting for her to finish so they could join the others for Spike's chowder. Lunch would be in the men's tent, since Tory's cabin had been declared temporarily off limits. Until the men set up another tent for Craig's stuff, the "lab" was her kitchen—and she was knee-deep in test tubes, syringes and the battery of electronic equipment scattered over the floor and drain boards.

"There," she announced, slipping the blood samples she'd collected into the centrifuge. Setting the timer, she started the machine spinning. "Once these are analyzed, you'll have everything you need for comparisons."

Craig looked quite pleased and backed up that satisfaction with a simple "Excellent."

"Why is it," Nick wondered aloud, "that you can blend all those chemicals and still not make a decent piecrust?"

Craig must have expected the kind of verbal sparring they'd been engaged in when he'd left. His bushy gray eyebrows dropped sharply, only to lift again in mild surprise.

Tory shrugged. "Beats me. You didn't seem to think the filling was too bad, though."

"Applesauce. It was great applesauce."

"Well, the puffins didn't mind the crust," she reminded him, and bent to disconnect the extension cord leading to her generator. She hated using that noisy thing. It always sounded as though it wanted to explode.

"True," Nick admitted. "But they liked your bread, too."

"You said my bread had potential."

"It does. It's a potential replacement for..."

"Steel?" she offered, and glanced up to meet the look she'd seen so often in his beautiful eyes.

Mixed with Nick's amusement was a look of hunger, respect and need. And something else that made her legs go predictably weak. She'd been seeing that look a lot lately.

What he saw in the way she held his eyes had been there a lot, too.

Clearing his throat, he reached for the cord she was coiling. "Let me do that. Your timer just went off."

Nick's last words were accompanied by the distinct whinny of a horse and sharp, staccato raps on her door. Moments later, Craig, rubbing his stiff leg—the limp he'd arrived with seemed to be growing more pronounced—was taking over Tory's task, and she was trying to calm Henry Nicoli.

Henry was the husband of Albert's and Katrina's very pregnant niece. From the panic-stricken look on his face and his not quite intelligible mix of English and Aleut, it sounded as though his wife was having her baby—right now. Tory knew that the girl had lost their first child in childbirth, so the panic the man was experiencing was more than just about-to-be-a-father nerves.

She darted toward the storage room, only to run right into Nick, who was coming out of it. Shoving her medical bag into her hands, he grabbed her jacket from its peg and pushed her out the door while she was absently nodding at his admonishment.

Four hours later, Tory wished she'd listened more closely to Nick's warning. "The barometer's been going crazy," he'd said, lifting her onto Henry's horse. "If you even think it looks like a storm's going to hit, you stay at their place until it passes." He hadn't let go of the reins until Henry had pointed out the general direction of his cabin. Nick's last words came back now with all the force of the wind surging around her. "I mean it, Tory. Stay there!"

Oh, Lord. If only she'd listened to him. It wasn't because she always got a little more headstrong when he told her what to do that had made her ignore what he'd said. It was just that in her excitement to tell him about the beautiful, healthy baby girl she'd delivered, she'd dismissed his warning along with any thought of the impending storm. It was only a little over a mile from the Nicolis' home to her cabin, and it hadn't even started to rain when she'd left almost an hour ago. Henry had offered her one of his horses, but she didn't know how to ride and Henry was too excited about his wife and daughter for Tory to accept his weaker offer to escort her back to her place.

It might not have been raining before, but it sure was now. The wind was so strong that the deluge felt like a zillion tiny needles stinging her face. The fact that she was drenched to the skin and so cold even her toenails felt as though they were shivering was bad enough. What made it all so irritating was the fact that she could barely see where she was going.

Her head was lowered more in an effort to keep the torrent of rain and ice pellets from blasting her face than to see where she was putting her feet. The grass was beaten flat and her boots seemed to have sprung a leak. Her hair was plastered against her head and rivulets of water kept running down her neck, even though her shoulders were hunched up. Why hadn't she brought a hat?

She should have put the lid down on the cold frame, too, she thought, sloughing her way through the river of mud. The carrots and radishes would probably be okay; it was the lettuce that was no doubt being pounded to a pulp.

Oh, come on, Tory, she chided herself, you're just trying not to think about how miserable you feel. Try to think about something productive, like how you're going to get changed and your hair dried before Nick shows up to say, I told you so.

For some reason, she had the feeling he wasn't going to be very pleased if he found out about this.

The wind picked up. She'd thought it couldn't possibly blow any harder, but suddenly she seemed to be pushing against a solid wall of air—and then she was lying on her back in the mud.

One thing about rain—it made the ground softer.

Lifting herself as well as she could after crawling a couple of feet to retrieve her bag, she started out again, practically doubled over against the force of the wind. And to think she used to like walking in the rain.

"Tory! Is that you?"

Squinting at the dim figure that appeared to be having as much trouble remaining upright as she was, she swallowed a defeated moan. "What are you doing out here?" she called back.

Nick didn't answer until his wet face was a few inches from hers. "I've got a better one," he retorted. "Where do you think you're going?"

"For a walk along the beach," she offered dryly, eyeing him through her glistening lashes.

His eyelashes had little drops of water clinging to their long ends. But what she noticed was the sarcasm dripping from his words when he muttered, "You were certainly headed in the right direction then."

"What?"

He pointed over her shoulder. "Your cabin's that way."

That took a bit of the flippancy from her tone. "It is?"

"Yes," he snapped. "It is. Damn it, Tory. I told you to stay where you were!"

"How did you know I hadn't?"

Taking her by the shoulders, he turned her around, pulled her against his side and started across the ground she'd just covered. "Just this feeling I had," he mumbled, not sounding terribly pleased with something so illogical.

"A feeling? You came looking for me because you had a feeling?"

"Don't push it, Tory."

He sounded angry. Angry and relieved, but mostly angry.

Tory hoped she sounded practical. "How are we going to get to the cabin?"

He quickened their pace when the wind abated for a few seconds and replied dryly, "By carrier pigeon."

Okay, she thought, I deserved that. "I mean, how are we going to find it? I thought I was heading there, but we can't see a thing."

"I've got a compass."

"I thought you couldn't use a compass in a storm."

"That's electrical storms. Do me a favor, will you?"

"Sure. What?"

"Just shut up."

She thought it would be wise to comply.

Nine

Tory kept the requested silence. She didn't even comment when Nick pulled her around the side of the cabin and she saw that someone—probably Nick—had put the lid down on her cold frame. By the time he'd shoved her inside and hauled her into the bathroom, she decided she'd been quiet long enough.

"What do you think you're doing?"

"What does it look like I'm doing?" he muttered tightly, and proceeded to add her sweater and bra to the growing pile of wet and muddy clothes lying on the floor.

"Undressing me. But I can do it myself."

"Then take your pants off." Stepping back while he kicked off his boots, he whipped the plastic shower curtain aside and turned on the faucet. His soaked vest and shirt joined her sweater. "Get in."

"But—"

"Tory." The way he said her name was a warning she didn't think would be wise to ignore.

Nick no longer looked angry; he looked downright furious. She'd never seen him like that before and wasn't feeling adventurous enough to push him further. What she was feeling was cold. From the neck down, she was one solid goose bump.

Stepping under the warmth of the shower, she pulled the curtain closed.

Nick whipped it right back open. "Hold this."

He shoved a bottle of shampoo into her hands, and after adding his jeans, socks and jockey shorts to the clothes draped over the commode, he stepped in beside her.

"Nick, this shower isn't big enough for one person, let alone—"

"Be quiet and turn around."

"I can't! I told you this isn't big enough for two peo—"

Nick had quite effectively refuted her inability to maneuver by turning her around himself. The spray of water rushing over her head and down her face had made her last word trail off with a gasp and a sputter. "You're drowning me!"

"That's something you already tried to do yourself." A liberal amount of baby shampoo was dumped on her head. "Why in the hell didn't you listen to me? Don't you realize that people die in storms like these?"

There was nothing at all sensual about the way he lathered her head and shoved it back under the water. In fact, he seemed quite close to strangling the throat he was soaping along with her arms and shoulders.

His last question had left her mute. Even when he'd told her she was heading in the wrong direction when he'd found her, it hadn't occurred to her to be frightened. Not for a moment had she thought she was in any real danger.

Nick was muttering, sounding as though he was talking more to himself than to her, when he angled to the side and ran the bar of soap over her stomach and down her thighs, then started to lather himself. "You've got to appreciate the trouble the weather can get you into around here. The next time I warn you about it, you'd damn well better listen. You could have slipped and hit your head on a rock, or—"

"Been blown out to sea?" she suggested, remembering the gust of wind that had sent her sprawling.

"It's been known to happen," he shot back, mistaking her comment for flippancy. "I wish to hell you'd take this seriously."

"I am taking it seriously." As seriously as she could under the circumstances. She was staring at the foamy bubbles he was rubbing into the hair on his chest and under his arms. Even with him yelling at her, there was something very erotic about watching him wash himself. "And stop swearing so much."

Glowering at her through the steam, he lowered his head to within inches of her water-slicked face. "Considering what else I feel like doing to you, swearing is nothing." His soapy hands flattened on the wall above her shoulders. But instead of telling her whatever else he'd been thinking about doing, he just glared at her.

Tory tried to glare back but found the expression difficult to manage. Seeing him so obviously aggravated with her was a little unsettling—and very revealing.

"Damn it, Tory," he groaned, dragging her from the wall and crushing her in his arms. "You scared the holy hell out of me."

His hold on her was almost desperate, and the feel of his hard, slick body seemed to transmit that desperation through her every nerve and cell. He was angry, not because she hadn't listened to him, but because she'd frightened him. For him to have been that afraid for her, he must feel something far stronger than he'd ever admitted.

Was it possible that that something was love?

"I didn't mean to scare you," she whispered, clinging to the rigid muscles of his back. "I was just so anxious to tell you about the baby that I—"

He wasn't listening. And the way his mouth clamped over hers made any further explanation impossible.

If she'd sensed desperation in him before, what she sensed now was even more fevered. His tongue plunged beneath hers, then drew up to push against its tip, seeking to master and tame. Immobilizing her head with his hands, he pushed her back against the stall, trapping her with his body. Each thrust of his tongue seemed to fuel the primitive force driving him, and the pressure of his mouth grew harder.

Their lovemaking had always been so gentle, so tender, yet filled with an urgency made even stronger by that very gentleness. There was none of that tenderness now. Only something raw, something that made the shock waves more pronounced as they radiated downward from where his hand flattened her breast. The way he pushed his hips against her stomach was an insistent demand, echoed in his savage domination of her mouth and the urgency of his fingers digging into her soft flesh.

The muscles in his sides flexed beneath her arms. A moment later the shower was off, the curtain shoved back, and he'd swung her off her feet.

Stunned by Nick's abruptness, she barely had time to realize that they were both still dripping wet before his hard length pressed her into the lush fur coverlet on her bed and he'd claimed her lips again. His kiss was fierce, filled with possession. Though it seemed to last forever, it was all too brief.

The terse imprecation he directed at himself was almost inaudible. The tortured expression darkening his face when he lifted his head spoke volumes. He'd been seeking to punish, and what she saw in his eyes was a betrayal of desire and self-disgust. Droplets of water joined the ones clinging to her shoulders when he shook his damp head. "I'll hurt you."

Locking her hands around his waist, she drew back the weight he was lifting from her. He was telling her he wouldn't take her in anger, but she knew what lay behind that fury. He was a man who needed to claim what he thought he might have lost. She was a woman who needed very much to show him she was his to claim.

Touching the rigid line of his jaw, she whispered, "You won't hurt me," and felt him tense when she curled her smooth leg over his rough one. Her light caress moved to the pulse hammering in his throat, then drifted to his shoulders. When he made no effort to pull away, she pushed him to his back.

Either he was willing to calm himself down or her soothing touch was having the desired effect. The nibbling kisses she placed on each of his flat nipples and repeated down the length of his abdomen were having the desired effect, too. The tension she could feel building beneath her hands was infinitely different from that driving him only moments ago. Anger and fear had nothing to do with the way his muscles constricted as her fingers feathered over his chest, or his sharp intake of breath when her lips drifted lower.

The clean scent of soap and his warm skin filled her lungs. Every breath seemed to conduct that essence through her body, drugging her, demanding more, making her ignore his husky appeals to stop. The provocative lift of his hips and the feel of his hands tangling in her hair refuted his words. The sound of her name being whispered so thickly only encouraged her loving caress.

"Tory," he rasped again, taking her by the wrists. He pulled her hands above her head and pushed her over. A tight, "No more," was breathed against her cheek and he started stringing a chain of slow, moist kisses along the curve of her neck.

There seemed to be a certain restraint guiding him, a deliberate effort on his part to hold himself back. The tips of his fingers floating down her side made her feel like something fragile. The way he stroked her, grazing the undersides of her breasts with his lips before suckling their darker centers, was all the more exquisite for his roughness before. She strained toward him, wanting to feel his weight. But her attempts to draw him to her were gently defied. Keeping her hands pressed into the pillow, Nick pinned her leg with his and continued the path his mouth was weaving over her ribs and across her stomach.

Each flick of his tongue on her skin coiled the knot growing inside a little tighter. Every brush of his fingers created a sensual friction designed to carry her further and further from the confines of reality. Her movements grew restless. His restraint vanished. She heard the moan come deep from within his chest, and the gentleness was gone.

He'd lifted himself over her, his mouth now bruising hers as he pushed his hand beneath her hip. The raw, primitive need was back. It was there in the force of his kiss, the feel of him entering her warmth, and the way her own body arched to take him. Yet, it wasn't an act of domination. Each thrust seemed to speak of a need far beyond possession or physical passion. Tory matched that urgent rhythm, giving as she received, and together they entered that place where nothing existed but the two of them. A place only they could share.

It seemed to take a long time for Tory to notice anything of substance. First, it was the feel of soft fur curving around her sides and the delicious heaviness of his body. Then, she realized how tightly Nick was holding her. He didn't seem to want to let go. She didn't want to, either.

"Are you all right?" she whispered, stroking his back.

He nodded, his chin feeling a little scratchy as it brushed her shoulder before he lifted his weight to his elbows. With one finger he lifted the strands of tangled hair from her forehead. "I think the question should be, are you?"

"Never better," she sighed.

He didn't look particularly convinced. "Tory, I didn't mean to act like that. I don't know—"

A silencing finger was placed over his lips. "It's okay," she assured him softly. "Honest."

There had been hesitancy in his searching eyes only a moment ago. Now there was relief and a hint of a smile. "I had a feeling you'd say that."

"Another feeling?" She made her own smile teasing in a deliberate attempt to quell the anticipation surging in her heart. "The same kind of feeling that made you come looking for me when I didn't even know I was lost?''

Rolling to his side, he propped his head on one hand and caressed her cheek with the other. ''I'm not sure what made me do that. Some kind of telepathy, I guess.''

That telepathy was something she'd noticed a long time ago. She wondered how strong it was, or if there was even really anything to it. Maybe a little test was in order.

Watching him while he traced her cheekbone, she put all her mental power into the three words she so longed to say.

Couldn't he see how deeply she cared for him?

Apparently he couldn't. All he seemed to see was the flicker of disappointment in her deep brown eyes a few seconds later. ''What's the matter?'' he asked with a slight frown.

''Nothing really. I was just trying to see if you could read my mind.''

''Read your mind?'' He chuckled. ''How could I possibly do that?''

''I guess you can't, but there've been times when it seemed like you could.''

''It's an interesting thought. But since we both know it's impossible—'' his hand curved over her hip and he lowered his head to brush his lips over hers ''—I think you'll have to verbalize your mental message.''

His touch was so tender, the soft inquiry in his eyes so compelling. Just a while ago he'd allowed her to see a part of himself he'd kept from her for so long, the part of him that acknowledged how much he needed her.

It was because of those things that she heard the words being spoken before she could pull them back. "I love you, Nick."

For a moment, everything went absolutely still. His hand stopped the ascent it had begun up her side. His lashes didn't blink or lower as he stared down at her. Even the pulse at the base of his throat seemed to have stopped.

Then, his hand moved and his lashes lowered. The pulse jumped in the hollow at the base of his neck, and seconds later she was staring at his back.

"I'd better go tell the guys you're safe." Reaching for the robe draped across the foot of the bed, he handed it to her. "They were worried about you. Oh, yeah," he added, heading into the bathroom. "They had bets going. Which was it? A boy or a girl?"

He wanted to know the sex of the Nicolis' baby? Now?

She pushed the word past the knot in her throat. "Girl. Nick—"

The closing of the bathroom door cut her off.

Dear God! What had she done?

Wrapping her heavily quilted robe around her to ward off the chill that seemed to be coming more from inside than anywhere else, she hurried into the hall.

The bathroom door opened and Nick didn't even look at her as he carried his clothes to the stove. He'd already pulled on his still very soggy jeans. She could only imagine how awful they must feel.

"Where are you going?" she managed in a voice so strained it didn't even sound like her own.

"Back to camp."

"But you'll get wet!"

"My clothes are already soaked," he muttered, and stuffed his arms into his very damp shirt sleeves. Not bothering with the buttons, he yanked on his vest and pulled on his socks. At least they looked dry. "Sounds like one of your shutters is coming loose."

She ignored his almost-conversational observation. "Nick, can't we—"

The look in his eyes stopped her cold. It was a plea for silence, tempered only by something that looked very much like pain. But the pain vanished along with the plea and his expression was as enigmatic as ever. "Just leave it, okay? I'll check that shutter on my way out. You've got clinic tomorrow, don't you?"

She didn't know what that had to do with anything, but she nodded anyway and shoved her fingers through her tangled hair. The subject she wanted so badly to discuss had clearly been posted off limits.

"I'll have somebody come up in the morning and clear out this equipment." He motioned to the stuff strewn around behind him. "You've got little enough space here as it is. A girl, huh?"

Again she nodded, not even bothering to dwell on the number of topics he'd covered in the past thirty seconds—or how he was so clearly dismissing the words she wished she'd never spoken.

That familiar little half smile of his didn't come anywhere near his eyes when he finished tying his boots and glanced back at her. "That means I lost."

That was the last thing he said before he bent his head against the driving rain and walked out her door.

The time Tory had wished so fervently she could harness while she and Nick had been together now seemed to drag by with all the speed of a geriatric turtle. Why was it that the Fates had decided to honor her request now? She needed time to go faster, not slower! It would be months before Albert's oldest son would return to the village and she could leave, and the thought of enduring Nick's icy silence for that long was almost more than she could bear. In the past three days, he'd said only one word to her. That had been a tight "Hi" when she'd passed him on her way to the tent the men had erected next to their sleeping quarters for Craig's lab.

Seeing him had made it very hard to concentrate on the work she'd tried to do in the lab that afternoon.

She tried everything she could think of to keep her mind off the dull ache that simply refused to go away. If only she still had a few of the bricks left in her emotional wall, something to hide behind so she wouldn't have to feel the hurt of his rejection. Playing with Willy and his dog hadn't helped. Neither did going to visit Katrina and listening to Albert's tales about his ancestors. Even her visit to Anna Dorvak and the clinic she'd held on Monday hadn't provided enough of a diversion. It didn't matter that Nick was deliberately making himself scarce. Tory was convinced that whoever had come up with the adage "out of sight, out of mind" must have been out of his. She didn't have to see Nick to think about him. He was always there in her mind, along with the questions she simply couldn't answer.

Why had he shut her out so completely? Why should telling him she loved him have made such a difference? Why wouldn't he talk to her? Why didn't she have the nerve to go and talk to him?

Because you're not a masochist, she told herself, providing at least one answer to the growing litany of questions. Then she glanced around when she heard Craig announce himself with a cheerful "Good morning!"

Unable to match his ebullience, she gave him a tiny smile and watched while he hobbled to the chair next to the equipment-loaded tables. The lab's catalytic heater sat a few feet from the chair and he angled his bad leg toward it.

It must have started snowing. There were a few melting flakes in his graying hair and dusting the shoulders of his quilted gray jacket. He didn't seem to notice.

"Have you got the cell-differentiation counts yet?" he asked.

At her nod he immediately launched into a dissertation about how he wanted to draw samples of the men's blood on a weekly basis and set up the graphs that would enable him to see the changes for comparison against the men's behavior patterns.

Craig's study was the one thing Tory could rely on to absorb her thoughts completely. The work was fascinating, Craig's theories were remarkable and she loved every second of what she was doing. Her analytical skills had always been good—on a professional level anyway—but she was beginning to discover a talent in herself she'd never explored before. Maybe that was why her expression grew so animated while she listened to him and, at his encouragement, tossed out a few ideas of her own.

It was almost two hours before she realized the thoughtful way Craig was considering her. Thinking he was getting ready to comment on something she'd just said, she wasn't prepared for his quiet observation.

"You've only got nine more months here, don't you?" The question was rhetorical and he didn't wait for a response before he threaded his fingers together and, slumping in his chair, splayed them across his chest. "Too bad."

His comment, though a little off-the-wall, was a direct reversal of her opinion on that particular subject. "Why's that?" she returned. Pulling her cabled beige sweater over the hips of her jeans, she leaned against the table.

"It's not going to be enough time. Would you be interested in a long-range commitment to this study?"

"How long-range?"

"About two and a half years. I don't think my leg's going to allow me to stay through the winter, Tory. Every time the temperature drops another degree, the thing starts aching even more. Fifty-year-old bones don't heal as fast as younger ones, you know."

"I know." She smiled, then tucked her bottom lip between her teeth.

"So, how about it? You interested?"

Giving her lip a pull, she sighed. "Under any other circumstances I would be, Craig. I'm flattered that you—"

"I'm not trying to flatter you." His interruption was uncharacteristically impatient. "You're good. Better than good. I need someone like you who can observe and do the tests. We could communicate by radio to discuss the interpretations and I'd come back for the summers. Besides that, with me gone, the men won't have a doctor after you leave and they move the base." Grasping the back of the chair, he winced when he tried to put his weight on his leg. "Just tell me you'll think about it," he requested, and limped toward the flap of the tent.

The way he'd grimaced at the pain in his leg made Tory wince, too. He'd also just provided her with an excuse not to reply to his request. "Try to keep that leg warm and keep it elevated as much as you can."

"Yes, doctor," he returned with an obedient nod. "And in return for that advice, I'll offer some of my own. I suggest you and Nick iron out your differences before you let whatever's going on between you two go any further. The rest of the men are already contemplating mutiny as it is. He hasn't exactly been easy to live with the last few days." Pushing aside the flap to let himself out, she heard him mutter, "Think I'll go light a fire under that guy."

A fire's probably what it's going to take, she silently grumbled. Nick's attitude toward her had been positively glacial.

She dropped into the chair Craig had just vacated and curled her fingers around her upper arms. One of them was going to have to break the ice, so to speak. It might as well be her. There was no way she was going to spend the rest of her time here witnessing a one-man enactment of the rebirth of the Ice Age. Nick Spencer was a hypocrite. Only last month he'd been ready to fire Mike for not concentrating on his job because of a woman. Now Nick was taking his frustrations, or whatever it was, out on his men for that very same reason.

Mike's problem had solved itself. About the time he'd decided he was going to stay with the expedition, he'd got a letter from his girlfriend telling him she'd become engaged to the local grocer.

Nick's problem was going to be solved by Tory.

They'd shared too much, been through too much,
for him to treat her like this. Okay, so she loved him,
mind, heart and soul. There wasn't a darn thing he
could do about that, any more than there was anything she could do to make him feel that way about
her. But she loved him enough not to ask for what he
so apparently couldn't give. He hadn't given her a
chance to tell him that, but it was something she had
to do.

Preferring activity to sitting there trying to figure
out just how she was going to do that, she started to
recheck the results of the tests she and Craig had run.
It was better to think about work anyway.

"Am I interrupting anything?"

The empty test tube she'd picked up clattered to the
table. She hated tents! There was no way a person
could knock on canvas!

Though every muscle in her body had tensed at the
sound of Nick's voice, she forced herself to resume her
task and put the tube in its rack.

"Craig wanted me to talk to you," Nick continued
when she hadn't answered or bothered to turn around.
"Do you have a minute?"

If Craig had sent Nick, that meant he hadn't come
on his own. "Sure," she replied with a shrug, keeping
her back to him. "But if he sent you to talk to me
about the job he offered—"

"There's a lot more to it than that, Tory," he cut in
tightly. "Would you please stop playing with those
things and turn around?"

"I'm not playing." And I don't want to turn around
because I don't think I can handle looking at you, she
added to herself. Having him this close was bad

enough. The thought of seeing the coolness she was so certain would be in his eyes was almost unbearable.

No. The feel of his hands settling on her shoulders was more than she could handle. "Nick, please—"

"I won't talk to you unless I can see you."

Before she could think of anyplace else to look, she'd met the eyes she so wanted to avoid. But what she saw there wasn't cool or remote at all. There was a wealth of anxiety and apology and longing betrayed in those compelling aquamarine depths. She caught only a glimpse of those heart-stopping emotions before the sweep of his ridiculously long lashes lowered in a slow blink. Now all she could see was a discordant mix of determination and uncertainty.

She could certainly identify with that last feeling. "What do you want to talk to me about?"

The muscle forming the cleft in his chin jumped. "I want to offer you a job," he said, sounding awfully defensive, and Tory felt her heart sink when his hands slipped to his sides. "Actually, it's more like three jobs."

Tory could think of only two he could possibly offer. It was a cinch that the third job wasn't as camp cook. And since his reason for being here only concerned work, there was no need for him to be standing so close. Didn't he know how hard it was for her not to reach up and touch the little laugh lines around his eyes that looked so much deeper than they had before? He looked so tired.

"Three?" she repeated, curling her hand into a fist.

He nodded and drew in a breath that stretched his sky-blue pullover more snugly over his broad chest. "It's sort of a package deal." The briefest hint of hesitation crept across his tense features, but he hurried on as if he was about to lose his nerve. "Craig's assistant. Camp doctor. And my wife. Not necessarily in that order."

Very slowly Tory sagged against the table. She knew what she'd just heard, but it didn't seem to want to register. The way her heart had just slid to her throat—the darn thing felt like a yo-yo—made it impossible to ask him to repeat himself.

Nick apparently thought she was preparing to say something he didn't want to hear. The agitated way he drew his hand through his windblown hair and the determination she heard in his voice only confirmed that supposition. "Just listen to me before you say anything. Okay?"

When he saw her nod, he started to pace between the tent flap and the chair by the heater. "I kept telling myself that if we didn't actually say anything, I could let you go when your year was up. I'd almost managed to convince myself that would work, until you opened your mouth, and these past few days... these past few days," he repeated with a rueful shake of his head. "I spent the first two trying to tell myself I wasn't really in love with you and the past twenty-four hours trying to figure out some way to keep us together. There's no way I want you living apart from me, but I'm committed to this expedition for the next two and a half years."

He wasn't looking at her. If he had, he would have known that he didn't have to continue pleading his case.

"We need to be together," he went on, sounding as though he was trying to convince her of something she was prepared to dispute. "Right now, the only way for that to happen is for you to stay on with the crew. It's the only alternative we've got. I know it'll mean more work for you, at least until Albert's son gets here—"

"I think I can handle it."

"But I'd help as much as I—" He bit his words off abruptly. Spinning around, his eyes froze on the smile dancing in hers. "What did you say?"

Clamping down the urge to fling herself in his arms, she calmly placed herself in front of him and tipped her head back. "I said, I think I can handle it."

The relief just beginning to drain the tension from his features was contradicted by the way his heavy brows lowered. "Which part?"

"I thought you said it was a package deal."

"It is," he confirmed with his knee-weakening little half smile. Or maybe it was the feel of his arms slipping around her waist and pulling her to him that caused her to lock her knees so she wouldn't fall through the canvas floor. "Say yes, Tory."

He hadn't given her a chance to say much of anything at all yet. And he wasn't allowing her to say anything now. The tender brush of his lips over hers was a mute repetition of the gentle command he'd just issued. He knew she hated it when he told her what to do. But this time he'd softened his command with the kiss that told her how much he needed for her to comply.

She didn't feel any need to rebel. What she did feel was an overwhelming need for the man whose love was a perfect counterpart to her own.

"For God's sake," he whispered, trailing a line of kisses from her mouth to her ear, "answer me."

His caresses had always left her a little disoriented. "What was the question?" she ventured, and heard him groan at her teasing.

"I asked you to marry me."

Snuggling her head against his chest, she buried a smile of contentment, wonder and joy in the soft knit of his sweater. "Do I get to think about it?"

"No!"

She tried to look displeased. It was a little hard to do when she was grinning like this, though. "Why not?"

"Because," he returned with a grin of his own.

" 'Because' is a lousy reason."

"Then, how about because I love you?"

"That's better," she conceded, and started to put her head back on his chest.

Nick's grip on her upper arms pulled her away. "Come on, Tory. Don't do this to me." The smile left his eyes. "I know I'm asking a lot, and the next couple of years won't be easy. Just ride this out with me, and as soon as we're finished here, we'll go any place you want. California. Maine. You name it. I can get a consulting job, or even teaching doesn't sound so bad anymore. Maybe we could—"

She touched her finger to his lips, silencing him with the love shining in her eyes. "We'll have plenty of time to work out the details," she assured him softly, and reached up to meet him in a kiss that told him it didn't matter where they went—as long as they were together.

You won't want to miss a single one of the heart-felt stories presented by Silhouette Special Edition; and when you take advantage of this special offer, you won't have to.

You'll also receive a FREE subscription to the Silhouette Books Newsletter as long as you remain a member. Each lively issue is filled with news on upcoming titles, interviews with your favorite authors, even their favorite recipes.

To become a home subscriber and receive your first 4 books FREE, fill out and mail the coupon today!

Silhouette Special Edition®

Silhouette Books, 120 Brighton Rd., P.O. Box 5084, Clifton, NJ 07015-5084

Silhouette Desire

COMING NEXT MONTH

OUT OF THIS WORLD—Janet Joyce
When Adrienne met Kendrick, she thought he was an alien from outer space. He insisted he wasn't, but how could she believe him when his mere touch sent her soaring to the heavens?

DESPERADO—Doreen Owens Malek
Half Seminole Indian, Andrew Fox had chosen the dangerous life of a bounty hunter. As a student of Indian folklore, Cindy found him fascinating—as a woman, she found him irresistible.

PICTURE OF LOVE—Robin Elliott
It didn't take Steve long to realize Jade was the woman for him, but Jade was a compulsive overachiever. Could she manage to temper her ambition and make room for love?

SONGBIRD—Syrie A. Astrahan
Desirée had to choose—her career as a disk jockey in California or Kyle Harrison, the man she loved, in Seattle. Could she possibly find the best of both worlds?

BODY AND SOUL—Jennifer Greene
Joel Brannigan fought for what he wanted, and he wanted Dr. Claire Barrett. She was ready for a fair fight, but Joel didn't fight fair...and he always won.

IN THE PALM OF HER HAND—Dixie Browning
Fate had thrown Shea Bellwood and Dave Pendleton together under rather bizarre circumstances, but who can argue with fate—especially when it leads to love.

AVAILABLE NOW: